THE KING AND THE KINDERGARTEN TEACHER

THE REBEL ROYALS BOOK 1

SHANAE JOHNSON

THOSE JOHNSON GIRLS

Copyright © 2019, Ines Johnson. All rights reserved.

This novel is a work of fiction. All characters, places, and incidents described in this publication are used fictitiously, or are entirely fictional. No part of this publication may be reproduced or transmitted, in any form or by any means, except by an authorized retailer, or with written permission of the author.

Edited by Alyssa Breck

Manufactured in the United States of America
First Edition February 2019

*I*n the view from his window, Leo looked out and saw the spires of tall castles. Tall towers of metal and glass dotted the landscape. Looking up, giant beasts roared and left trails of smoke in the early morning sky. Multicolored lights flashed in the distance like a witch or wizard casting a spell. Down below in the street, life-sized animals waved hello to awed children and posed for rowdy passersby.

New York City's Times Square was pure magic.

Leo wanted to go down and be a part of it. But that would be impossible. Duty called. It always did, which was why he rarely had a good night's sleep.

He might live in a palace full of servants. Their main job might be waiting on him hand and foot. But each one of those people were ultimately his responsibility. As their monarch, their livelihoods were in his hands.

"Are you ready for your speech, your majesty?"

King Leonidas turned away from the revelry below him. He dusted off the formal suit and coat of arms over his chest. He might hold a title. He might know how to wield a sword.

But there were no fairytales or romance in modern nobility. No. It was all business and protocol.

"It's important to bring up Cordoba's ample resources," said Giles who was serving both as his valet and chief of staff while on this trip to New York. "That will attract more business interest."

"Yes, I know." Leo moved to the standing mirror in the suite to straighten his tie.

But Giles brushed his hands away and undid the perfectly straight knot. "It would be most advantageous if we could capture the Spanish government's interest. Their resources pair perfectly with ours. It would be a match made in heaven. In fact, that's not the only match that would benefit our two countries."

Leo rolled his eyes. Unfortunately, Giles didn't catch the gesture. The man was far more focused on making the noose around Leo's neck even more pretty.

It had been two years since Leo's first wife had died. Giles wasn't the only one after him to choose a new bride. The whole country was antsy for a new queen, and Leo was starting to feel the pressure.

He might feel responsible for each citizen in his country. But did that give them all the right to have a say in his personal life? Being in the Land of the Free, Leo wondered if democracy wasn't the way to go over a monarchy.

He looked again out at the bright lights of the big city. If he were just another citizen, he'd be free of his duties, and he could live his life. He could go out to Times Square. He could attend a sporting event without disrupting the whole country. He could have a cup of coffee in a shop tucked away in a corner. He could ask a girl out for said cup of coffee—unchaperoned. He was a thirty-year-old king and, for much of his life, he still had to be chaperoned by aides and security.

Cordoba was a small island country in the Mediterranean between the southwestern border of France and the northeastern border of Spain. It was virtually unheard of here in America. Therefore, his security detail and entourage were at a minimum. Just Giles and a driver most days. He could slip them easily enough. He'd seen his brother do it many a time.

Leo turned from the window and picked up the notes for his speech. He knew thousands of people were relying on him for their livelihoods. So he did his duty. And he would do this duty of finding a new wife. Eventually.

He couldn't ask out a random woman for coffee. Just like his first marriage, his second would be a transaction. Not of the heart but of national interests.

"The Spanish duchess, Teresa of Almodovar, comes highly recommended. She's young, educated, philanthropic, and the women in her family's breeding history are quite positive."

Leo would've cringed if he hadn't heard this litany before with his first wife. Isabel had all these same qualities, and they'd gotten along amiably. But that was as far as the fires of passion rose.

He'd never experienced passion. He never would. It wasn't in the cards for a king.

Leo gave his collected notes a shuffle. He knew them all by heart. What was in his cards was economic stability and a wife who would satisfy an industrial need and breed an heir. If they managed to get along, as he and Isabel had, that would be a perk but not a requirement.

"It's been two years," said Giles. "Ample time for a respectful mourning period. Cordoba needs an heir."

"I already have a child."

"You know our country's constitution is patriarchal." Giles held up his hand before Leo could argue. "We don't have time or support to change that law. You'll need to find a new queen and produce a male heir. Otherwise ... I don't want to consider the alternative."

As if he heard them talking about him, the alternative bumbled into the room. A slightly younger, much more straggly version of Leo opened the door and spilled into the room.

Alex's shirttails were untucked. His belt was missing. His collar was askew with visible lipstick on the white fabric. Alex had likely made his way up from the revelry of Times Square.

Leo didn't envy his brother his playboy ways. He did envy that his brother had more choices in who he could love. Not that his brother opted for any choices. Alex was of the opinion of why choose when he could have them all.

"Good morning, your highness," said Giles, his tone drool, his emphasis on morning.

"Is it morning already? I was hoping to catch a few winks before the sun came up." Alex shaded his eyes from the dawning daylight. "Too late. There it is."

"You didn't sleep at all?" asked Leo.

"Oh, I slept a little. Just not in my own bed." Alex pulled off his jacket. And in true rakish fashion, he let it fall where it may on the floor, secure in the knowledge that someone would pick it up. "You don't need me for anything today? No ribbons to cut? No heiress to entertain? No press to distract with my insanely photogenic mug?"

"Actually," said Leo. "I do have need of you. You promised to take Pen out today."

Alex blinked, as though waking from a long slumber. "I did?"

Leo nodded. "On a tour of a local school. She wanted to see a kindergarten class."

"Fine." Alex sighed dramatically and scrubbed a hand over the scruff of his face. "The little pea is the only woman I keep my word to. I just need a catnap. And a shower. And a change of clothes. And then I'll be good as new."

Alex slumped on the couch. He closed his eyes and was out in the same instance. The man had always had the ability to slip into a contented sleep wherever he lay his head. That was easy when you didn't have a care in the world.

Leo put his notecards back in order and placed them in his coat pocket. Before leaving, he poked his head into his daughter's room. She was the little woman his loyalty flocked to first. Aside from his duty to his people, his daughter was his reason for everything.

Princess Penelope slept peacefully in the hotel room bed. Her dark hair fanned out over the white pillow case. A book of fractions lay on the side table.

Unlike most five-year-olds, his Pen preferred to fall asleep doing mathematics. It was a trait she'd received from her mother. Isabel had studied engineering at university even though she knew she'd never be able to use it in her duties as queen. It had made his wife happy. Numbers made his little girl happy, so he was more than happy to pick up a pencil and do algebra at bedtime in lieu of a story.

Losing her mother at such a young age was hard for his Penelope. He should've left her home, but he hated being parted from her. She was the true love of his life.

His angel slept soundly. He didn't dare wake her even though he wanted to say good morning before starting his day. He was beginning his day early, and he didn't want to throw her schedule off. Especially with her uncle knocked out in the other room.

Penelope deserved a mother, and he would find her the best one possible. That would be his number one criteria. Not some economic advancement for his country. Instead, Leo would focus on the advancement of his daughter. With his resolve set, Leo headed out to curry favor for his country and find a mother for his daughter.

CHAPTER TWO

"And the charming prince drew his sword and rushed to rescue the princess when—"

"But, Ms. Pickett?"

Esmeralda Pickett looked up from the picture book at the interruption. This wasn't the first interruption of the story. She'd paused at nearly every page of the story to answer a question or offer an explanation to the bright-eyed kindergarteners in her class. She was proud of her inquisitive group. Their little minds were like sponges, hungry to soak up new knowledge.

"Ms. Pickett, why can't the princess draw her own sword?" Aubrey Thomas scrunched her button nose up as she tried to work out her problem with the story. "You said this wasn't the first prince to try to rescue the princesses. And they're all in the dragon's lair. So there are other swords lying around on the ground. Why doesn't she just pick one of those up herself?"

That was very good logic, especially from a five-year-old who Esme often suspected was going on fifty. All around Esme, ten other little heads bobbed and tilted their heads as they considered this addendum to the story. They didn't immediately look to Esme for the answer. No, they discussed the possibilities and parameters amongst themselves.

They'd been listening attentively for the first two pages. The interruptions had begun once the princess disobeyed her father and went into the woods. Esme's class gaped with wide eyes as though they had never considered disobeying their parents.

They gasped with open mouths and hands clutching at imaginary pearls when the princess accepted food from a stranger. A discussion group broke off between Kurt Willis and Carla Barrow about the dangers of accepting candy from strangers or anything that was not in a pre-packaged wrapper that had the ingredients and allergens clearly labeled for their moms and dads to read.

But the kicker had been Tracey Chen. She'd crossed her arms over her chest in abject horror, pigtails swaying with the movement when Esme had described the villain of the story as an evil witch and showed her picture. Tracey was certain that Esme was discriminating against the elderly and those with psoriasis and eczema.

What five-year-old even knew any of those words, could pronounce them and knew what they meant? But, hey, at least they were all engaged. And that's what learning was about. Wasn't it?

"Okay," said Esme, addressing the latest query posed to her by the youngsters. "What if the princess did pick up the sword? What do you think she'd do?"

"With the sword, the princess could slay the dragon herself," said Aubrey, as though it were the most natural thing in the world. "Then she could get home before bedtime, apologize to her parents, and not get too big of a consequence for her actions."

"But she slayed a dragon," said Carla. "That's animal cruelty." She was a vegan and cried every time she saw one of her classmates eating chicken fingers or hot dogs.

"Dragons aren't real," said Aubrey.

"They are in my culture," said Tracey. "In China, they symbolize strength and power and good luck. That's why my people wear them in parades."

Kurt Willis sniffled as though the thought of an imaginary dragon in pain or a costume dragon in a parade hurt him. "I think she should sit down and talk to the dragon and work out her problems with words."

"These are all very good ideas," said Esme. "But what do you think the prince should do?"

The class stared mutely.

"I'd forgotten about him," said Aubrey.

"Why is he there again?" asked Tracey.

"To rescue her, I think?" said Carla.

"But she made the problem," said Aubrey. "My mommy says if you get into a jam, you gotta clean it up yourself."

Esme believed it. Aubrey's mother was all standards and procedures. On the first day of school, Mrs. Thomas had shown up with a ten-page, hole-punched folder entitled Getting to Know Aubrey. In it was the bathroom cycle the child had been trained on since one-years-old, and Mrs. Thomas insisted Esme keep to it.

"In fairytales," said Esme, filling the silence, "it's the prince's job to rescue the princess and the damsels in distress."

"Damsels in distress?" both Tracey and Carla mouthed the new words as if hearing them for the first time.

"But this is the real world, Ms. Pickett," said Aubrey.

"There's a queen in England and a whole bunch of princesses."

"One's coming to visit us today," Carla bounced on her bottom.

"But she's just a little girl." Aubrey rolled her eyes. "My mother met a grown princess. She rescued children from war zones."

"Ooh," said Kurt. "Did you get to meet her?"

Aubrey nodded. "She brought me chocolates, but they had dairy so I couldn't have them."

All the kids turned and listened to Aubrey's story. And story time was effectively over. Esme closed the picture book.

"All right everyone," she said. "To your sleeping mats. It's nap time."

There was a chorus of groans, but they all did as they were told. Eventually. Kurt went to the cupboard to get his special blanket. Aubrey fished her earbuds and iPhone out of her cubby hole. A part of Aubrey's welcome packet said that she had to nap listening to Brain FM.

Finally, all the kids were down for their midmorning nap. The resource teacher came in relieving Esme for her lunch break, and boy did Esme need it.

She'd only been on the job for a couple of months, but these weren't your average kids. Back in undergrad, she'd dreamed of changing kids' lives, giving them a hunger for learning, and widening their imaginations. The only hunger she was allowed to quench at Global Learning Preparatory Academy had to be from pre-packaged, dairy-free, nut-free, gluten-free products. Imaginations were stifled because these kids didn't watch TV or play games that weren't educational. Esme wasn't changing anything.

She grabbed her purse from the teacher's lounge and

prepared to go out into the bright New York City day. Walking down the hall of the school, she passed awards, recognitions, and commendations. The kids of years past captured in the celluloid all looked serious. Not a single smile of joy or eyes sparkled with imagination.

Esme was still determined to bring fun and joy into her class' childhoods. But first, she needed a break. And some sustenance.

"Miss. Pickett."

Esme's shoulders drooped at the sound of Principal Clarke's voice. The way he said Miss was elongated with the buzzing sound of a Z in place of the double S. It was like he wanted to swat the extra S of her single hood away from her and put in a firmly rooted R to make her a Mrs.

Esme wanted that too. The problem was not many twenty-something men were ready to settle down. Thirty was the new time to get engaged. And don't even think about kids before thirty-five after the career was settled, the house built and feng shuied, furnished, and child proofed.

Like most things, Esme was a fan of the old ways. She was a feminist, to be sure. But the kind that wanted equal rights and pay and still have a man open the door for her and sweep her off her feet. She could put up a good fight next to her prince if a dragon—in a tower or in a parade— came after them. But why should she when he should be well-equipped to do it for her?

"Ms. Pickett, I just received another complaint about inappropriate reading material in your class. Something about princesses and dragons and swords?"

Esme whirled around. How had he known that? She'd just left her classroom.

"Aubrey Thomas's mother just called."

Aubrey-stinking-Thomas. The kid had a cell phone. Had

she texted her mom? Well, she could already read. Most of the five-year-olds in her class were on a second grade level already and were bored with her alphabet lessons.

"Parents entrust us to prepare their children for the real world, Miss. Pickett."

Did no one believe romance still existed in the real world? That there were men who would slay a dragon for their true love? Apparently not. Most men her age vanquished trolls by swiping left and leaving it at that.

"I believe you have a bright future here with us," said Principal Clarke. "But if I continue to receive calls ..."

"I was trying to teach a moral lesson," said Esme. "I just didn't get to the end of the story."

"Try a different story. Perhaps a biography next time?"

Esme breathed through her nose to keep her mouth shut. Facts, she felt, were for fourth graders.

"We have a very important visitor coming in today. The Prince and Princess of Cordoba. We want to make a good impression."

That's all anyone cared about at this school. Impressions. Not imagination.

"I'm going to grab a slice of pie," said Esme. "Can I bring you back something?"

"Pie? Carbs in the afternoon? My, my, you do live dangerously, Miss. Pickett."

With another deep breath through her nose, Esme kept her mouth shut and headed out of the building. She whipped her cell from her pocket, texting Jan to have a slice of her usual warmed up for her and on a plate by the time she rounded the block.

Esme hit SEND. When she looked up, she couldn't believe her eyes. There was a dragon in the middle of the street. And it was flying straight for her.

CHAPTER THREE

he city of New York passed by Leo in concrete gray, denim blue, and fluorescent lights as he looked out the car window. Passed by him was a relative term. He could walk faster than the car traveled in traffic. The busy street was more a parking lot than a thru way.

"Sorry it's taking so long, gents," said the driver.

He tipped his hat as he looked back at Leo and Giles in the back seat. Their driver was a New York native. He was tickled when he learned he'd be driving around a real live king. In fact, the man had actually giggled like a schoolgirl when he'd come face to face with Leo.

"That's quite all right," said Leo.

"Was that you said you want to quit, your royalness?"

Leo had traveled extensively before he was crowned. Back in his school days, he spent a good deal of time in Germany where he'd mastered the gruff language. After school, he did a lot of mission work in French-speaking Africa where the accents were thick.

He excelled at communication. Except here in New York where the tongue twisting accents, the double negatives, and the flipped meanings of words often threw him. And vice versa, so it would seem.

"No," said Leo. "I mean the traffic is not your fault."

The driver nodded. "Sorry, man. The way you speak English is all fancy. I have enough trouble understanding people from Jersey."

Leo laughed at that. Despite the miscommunication, he enjoyed the driver's chatting since picking them up from the airport. They would've had their own Cordovian driver, but the embassy said it would be better to have a native New Yorker navigating the streets this week when diplomats from all over the world would be clogging the throughways.

Leo looked out at those streets. What he wouldn't give just for a moment of freedom. A moment to disappear into the crowd.

"Why don't we just get out and walk?" said Leo.

Giles huffed as though something harsh and distasteful clawed its way from the back of his throat. "You're a king. A king does not walk. Especially in a foreign city."

"No one knows who I am here. I could be any regular Joe on the street."

Now Giles scrunched up his nose as though he smelled something truly foul. "You are from a line of great warriors and leaders the likes of which would've crushed these rebels when they dared disagree with their king centuries ago. You are far from regular."

Leo chanced a glance into the rearview mirror. "No offense," he said to the driver.

"None taken," said the driver. "I'm not exactly sure what he said."

Leo chuckled again, and then his stomach got in on the action. "What I am is famished."

"You had breakfast at the hotel suite." Giles didn't even look up. He shuffled the papers of his dossier.

"I'm hungry again," Leo complained, sounding very much like his five-year-old at bedtime.

"Of course, you are," Giles said under his breath but loud enough for Leo to hear. "We're nearly there. I'm certain there will be plenty for you to eat."

Though Leo wore the crown and sat on a throne, he felt his life had never been his own. Before it was Giles keeping him on a schedule, it was his parents dictating his every move. Sometimes he wondered if the castle in the sky where he resided was actually a gilded cage.

He turned again to the New York scenery. As they turned a corner, a castle came into view. Or the approximation of a castle. Instead of turrets, the awning resembled the crust of a plump pie. The sign above read *Peppers' Pies.*

Displayed outside the pie shop was a placard welcoming the many countries present for the UN General Assembly just a few blocks away. The car moved slow enough for Leo to read the day's specials. On the menu were Australian meat pies, Serbian bundevara pies, and ... could it be?

"Pull over," said Leo.

"Your majesty, we do not have time."

Leo looked at the dash. They still had a full hour before his speech. Giles simply liked to be extremely early for all events to head off any chance of catastrophe. Which there never was a single one.

"You can spare your king a moment to satisfy his most basic of needs."

Giles huffed again but relented.

The driver pulled over and parked directly in front of the pie shop. It wasn't exactly a legal parking spot, but their diplomatic tags afforded them leeway.

Leo reached for the door handle, but Giles beat him too it. The man hopped out of the car and was on the other side before Leo's feet had even touched the ground.

"No need for you to come in and cause a fuss," said Giles. "I can gather from the sign what you want. I'll place your order, and we can be on our way."

Leo's presence on the street may have caused a bit of a fuss back in Cordoba where people knew who and what he was. But here, on the streets of New York, no one gave him a half a glance. Still, Giles glared when Leo alighted from the car.

"I'm sure I'll be fine," said Leo.

"Allow me a modicum of humor," said Giles. "Will you wait near the car?"

"Fine," Leo said with a huff of his own. He could stand to be outside breathing the fresh stench-filled air for a few moments.

With one more huff, Giles turned and went inside.

Leo turned and looked around at the land of the free. He turned and tilted his head up at the sky. Looking up amongst the giant buildings, he felt small. Looking out amongst the sea of people, he felt insignificant.

A person brushed by him, bumping his shoulder. "Watch it," the person called back.

Leo didn't take affront. He'd never experienced rudeness to his face. It was a new experience, and he chose to laugh it off. Which didn't make the retreating person any happier. They scowled and continued walking.

A few women passed Leo. They eyed him up and down. The looks they gave him over their shoulders were come hither. He could've hithered. But, of course, he didn't.

Aside from being a father of a young girl, Leo had never been one for flings. Unlike his brother. All his life, Leo had been a one woman kind of man. And since he'd been engaged since birth, he had remained faithful to the one woman he made his promises to.

The only woman he'd ever kissed was his departed wife. The next woman he would kiss would have the same title and responsibility. It was simply his lot in life. One he accepted.

Leo turned back and faced the street. Traffic had lessened in the few minutes they'd been parked. Vehicles were moving near the speed limit once more. Except at the stoplights and pedestrian crossings.

At the street crossing directly ahead of him, a woman looked down at her phone. The walkers had cleared from the middle of the street and were safely on the side walk. But this woman wasn't paying heed to the red hand signaling her to stop. She was too focused on her phone.

A truck rounded the corner, moving at the speed limit. The woman continued to look down. From the angle, Leo could tell she was in the driver's blind spot. Neither saw the other.

Perhaps it was the warrior blood of his Moorish ancestors? Or maybe the adventurous spirit of his Conquistador forefathers? Perhaps the arrogance of the French aristocrats in his family tree kicked in. Whatever it was that set him in motion, Leo didn't think. He simply acted.

Leo dashed around the car and into the street. With just a second to spare, he placed his arms around the woman and yanked her to him. A split second later, the bumper of the truck occupied the space where she'd been. The force of Leo's tug and the impact of her body crashing into his sent them both to the ground.

The woman yelped in surprise. The brakes of the truck

squealed in protest. Leo grunted as he fell hard on his back with the woman on top of him.

"Oh, my gosh," breathed the woman. "Oh, my gosh. Oh, my gosh."

She looked up at the truck that was inches away from them. She looked down at Leo who was sprawled beneath her. It may have been the near death experience, but Leo could've sworn he saw stars sparkling over her head.

"Oy, you two love birds, take it inside and off the street," the truck driver shouted at them before turning his wheel and maneuvering around their entangled bodies.

The truck puttered away with a blast of exhaust. Leo covered the woman's face with his shoulder to protect her from the fumes. When the air cleared, he was left staring into the most dazzling, deep brown eyes he'd ever seen. It was a brown so dark it could almost be black, but there was a light at the center that radiated outward. For a moment, Leo was dazed.

"Death by dragon," she said.

He dragged his eyes from her lips. She wasn't wearing any lipstick, likely only Chapstick as her lips were glazed, and she smelled faintly of mint and cherries. "I beg your pardon?"

"I was nearly taken out by a dragon."

She looked in the direction of the departing truck. That's when Leo noticed the green dragon on the side of the truck detailing Dragon Dry Cleaning Services.

"You saved me," she said. "My own knight in shining armor."

"I'm no knight."

"You are in my book."

She grinned down at him, and he was once more at a loss for words. His gaze again fastened to her lips. And then, wonder of wonders, her pink tongue snuck out of the corner of her mouth to moisten her already glossed lips. Leo's hunger multiplied tenfold.

It took a series of honking horns to bring him back to the present and the danger that still plagued them. They remained in the middle of the street with cars arrowing to pass by their still entwined bodies.

His damsel pushed off his chest to right herself. Then she bent over and offered her hand to Leo. He stared at her offered hand for another full second, wondering how the roles had been reversed.

In the end, he took her hand in his. He didn't use any of her strength to help him to stand. He rose of his own accord. While doing so, he reveled in the touch of her flesh against his.

They moved to the sidewalk, still hand in hand. All too soon, she yanked her hand away from him. Then promptly patted his pants legs, dangerously close to the crown jewels.

"Oh, no," she said. "I've ruined your suit."

Leo looked down to see that there were smudges on the side of his coat and pant leg. It had been a long time since a woman had touched him. Even though she was brushing rather harshly.

"I was rushing," she said, her focus on the specks of dirt and grime on the fabric of his clothing. "Trying to order food on my phone. I'm on my lunch break, and I don't have much time. That's why I was looking down at my phone. And now I'm babbling. Is that your car?"

Leo was having trouble keeping up. He looked from the woman to her phone, back to her, and then to the car. "Yes."

"You know you can't park there. You'll get a ticket."

He shook his head. "Diplomatic immunity."

"Oh. Oh, I know that flag. It's the flag of Cordoba."

The orange, red and blue to represent the different countries from which the majority of Cordoba's people hailed. With his country's flag displayed prominently and proudly on the town car, Leo waved goodbye to his anonymity.

"Do you work for the prince?" she asked.

Without thinking, the truth came out of his mouth. "No, I am the king."

"Oh, you work for the king? How exciting."

Clearly, she'd misunderstood him. It must be the accent again. But Leo decided to go with it. A little thrill went through him that his anonymity was restored. "It's really not exciting at all. The king deals with the affairs of state. Agriculture, taxes, real estate."

"But you live in the castle? I'd love to hear more about it. Can I buy you a cup of coffee and a slice of pie as a thank you for the life-saving?"

A cup of coffee from a beautiful stranger? "Yes."

As they approached the door to the pie shop, Leo saw Giles frown at him. He gave the man a signal to keep his mouth shut. Giles glared, and Leo could hear the huff from across the room. But for once, the man did as he was commanded and kept his mouth shut. Even if it was pressed into a line of clear disapproval.

"I'm Esme, by the way."

"I'm Leo."

CHAPTER FOUR

Despite all the fairytales, romance novels and Hallmark movies Esme consumed, she'd never once considered herself the damsel in distress type. But man was it working for her right now. Esme had fallen into the arms of a real-life hero.

Technically, she'd crash landed into him while doing the most benign, stereotypical thing that a Millennial American could do. But who cares, because it paid off, and she was gonna live to tell this tale, and what a tale it was shaping up to be.

Leo held out his arm for her in a perfect right angle of chivalry. Just like in the BBC period films she'd watched on public television as a kid. She panicked for a second, uncertain exactly what to do.

Did she tuck her hand under his elbow and curl her fingers in the crook? Or lay her hand on top of his forearm, resting her fingers lightly? What had the actress who played Elizabeth done with Mr. Darcy in *Pride and Prejudice*? Not the Keira Knightley two-hour movie that played ad nauseam on cable. The delectably long, four-hour episodic one that played weekends during donation drives.

In the end, she decided she wanted some of that crook action. And so Esme just placed her hand between his ribs and his biceps. Her knuckles brushed against the fine coat she'd ruined with her epic absentmindedness. His coat was finer than her most expensive outfit. That wasn't saying much since she tended to shop at thrift stores and not on Fifth Avenue. But all thought left her when her fingertips met his bulging muscles.

And—oh, boy—what a bulge it was.

This man of the palace was no slob. There were more hills than valleys on his arm than in the Grand Canyon. She wondered what he did for the king? He had to be security, with that physique, and that serious face, and the hero skills.

Perhaps Captain of the King's Guard? Maybe he was a knight? In the storybooks, the men who protected kings were always knights. But he said he wasn't a knight. Still, he would forever be donned as her knight in shining armor.

And just to prove the point, he held the door for her and allowed her to precede him in. His head even bowed slightly as he allowed her to pass him. Esme's heart did a flip and a flop and crashed down into her ribs.

Oh, boy, was she in big trouble.

A man stood at the counter frowning at the two of them. He had the same golden tan and dark good looks as Leo. He was dressed similarly, but he was clearly older. Likely just a few years. There were no wrinkles in his face, but his eyes were alight with a weariness.

"I've decided to have my pie here, Giles," said Leo. "I know we're on a schedule and have to get to the UN for the King's speech. I won't take too much time."

Giles looked over Esme's head at Leo. Then he looked back down at her. If possible, his frown turned even more severe, as though he smelled something from the sewer. But he inclined his head. With one more glance at Esme, he left the take-out container of pie on the counter and headed toward the door.

"Sorry." Leo took a seat next to her at the counter. "Giles hates to be late."

"I don't want to keep you from your job." That was a lie. Yes. Yes, she did want to keep him.

"We have plenty of time to get there. Giles thinks if you're on time you're late."

"I don't have that much time myself. I'm only on a short lunch break. Even shorter now since my brush with death."

"What?"

They both turned to face the woman behind the counter. She slammed her hands down on the counter along with the exclamation. The pound was only a thud since her hands were covered in oven mitts.

Esme held up her hands in a calming fashion. "It was just a figure of speech, Jan."

"You're often prone to the dramatic, but it's always based on a modicum of truth." Jan knew Esme far too well. It was a condition that came with being best friends.

"When I was texting you, I wasn't watching where I was going and stepped into traffic."

Jan's eyes went as wide as a rounded pie tin.

"Thankfully, Leo here saved both my life and my phone from certain disaster."

"I swear, Esme, you always have your head in the clouds. You need to keep your feet, and your eyes, on the ground."

Jan slid a slice of pie toward Esme. The crust was darkened with black streaks, and green filling spilled out of the sides. "Speaking of near-death experiences, here's your poisoned apple pie."

Esme rubbed her hands together, preparing to dig into her favorite meal.

"Poison?" Leo asked, his face contorted in horror. But even with the grimace, he was still devilishly handsome.

"Oh, it's a joke," Esme clarified. "I'm named after a princess."

Something shifted in his features. Esme couldn't quite tell if it was surprise or dismay.

"Princess Esmeralda, most notably in Disney's *The Hunchback of Notre Dame.*"

"I know the story," he said. "But she didn't eat an apple. And she wasn't a princess. She was a commoner."

Esme shrugged. "Poetic license."

Again, his look went inscrutable.

"I suppose this is for you?" Jan took the boxed up pie out of its container and placed it on a plate.

Spices from a foreign land tickled Esme's nose. The heat of the spices warmed her cheeks. The sweetness of the scent tickled her tongue, enticing her to ask for a bite.

"This is why I pulled over," said Leo. "I couldn't resist your ploy of authentic Cordovian fare. This looks and smells just like a bisteeva."

He dug in and took a bite. His eyes rolled into the back of his head, which was a common occurrence here in Jan's bakery.

"It tastes just like the palace cook's bisteeva," Leo said, taking another bite. "No, better. Please, don't tell him I said that."

Jan grinned ear to ear facing another convert to her culinary ways.

"Leo, this is my best friend and the maker of the best pies in the world, Jan."

"Hello, Jane."

"No, it's Jan," Jan corrected. "No E. I'm too plain to be even a Jane. Just Jan."

Leo dropped his fork and held out his hand to Jan. Jan held out her oven-mitted hand to him for a shake. Leo grinned and turned her oven-mitted hand palm side up and planted a kiss on the daisy covered fabric.

"Wow," said Jan. "That's new."

Wow indeed. Esme hadn't gotten a hand kiss. She'd never had a guy do that for her. She dreamed about it enough. She supposed Leo might've done that to her, had she been right side up when they'd met.

"Have you visited Cordoba?" Leo asked.

"I haven't visited anywhere," said Jan. "I've just always had a knack for spices. Those little cloves, corns, and flowers can transport your taste buds around the world and back for a fraction of the price."

Leo nodded. "The almonds are as sweet as if you plucked them straight from a tree in Majorca. The cumin is warming my mouth as though I'm laying out in the Mediterranean. And you used actual squab instead of chicken."

"I'm surprised you can tell the difference."

"You have a gift."

Leo took another bite of his pie. He closed his eyes and groaned in delight. There was no music playing in the pie shop. All that could ever be heard was a chorus of happy groans from the customers. It was the music to Jan's ears.

Jan glanced at Leo, then at Esme. Her staunchly single friend gave Esme an approving smile before moving aside to serve another customer. Esme turned her attention to her own slice. She took a bite as she thought of a topic of conversation to hold the interest of the man who sat beside her.

"So, Leo, what's the king of Cordoba like? Is he old, and prone to madness like King Lear? Is he a bumbling idiot like Jasmine's father in Aladdin? Or is he off with his head like the Queen of Hearts in Alice in Wonderland?"

"You have quite the imagination."

"It's my curse."

"I like it." He downed the last of his pie, closing his eyes as he slowly pulled the prongs of the fork from his mouth.

Esme was mesmerized. Oh, to be one of those four prongs.

"You're completely wrong about modern monastic rule though," he said.

"I beg your pardon?"

"About the modern monarchy. Running a kingdom is very much like running a Fortune 500 company, only harder."

"How so?"

"Back in ancient and medieval times, kings were considered God's representative on earth. They owned land and often the people on that land. Over time, their power became limited by feudal nobles because they couldn't manage the vast amounts of land and resources on their own. Later, they came to rely on the church for assistance. Though most often than not, they were strong-armed by the papacy. Kings took an oath to keep the peace, administer justice, uphold the laws, and protect the poor who resided on their land. Democracy grew as people became autonomous, but the influence of the king remained strong in many lands."

That was a delightful history lesson. But she failed to see the point. "So what does the king actually do?"

"In this age, the kings and queens of nations delegate their power so that the police keep the peace, the courts dispense with justice, and the governments deal with lawmaking. And in some monarchies, they're simply figureheads."

"In Cordoba?"

"In Cordoba, I'd like to believe that the king leads. But he doesn't do it on his own. There is a parliament."

"Like in England? So the king does more than just takes photos and comes out on holidays?"

"Yes, but he also brokers business deals for the country's industries. He makes deals with their resources. He's very much in charge of the economy, even with the law makers at the helm. Cordoba has a long history with the king playing an active role. That continues today."

"He sounds like a great man," said Esme. "Not quite the stuff of fairytales."

"The nobility of reality has never mirrored what is in the storybooks. Those of royal blood typically marry others of royal blood. You only ever hear about the exceptions like the Windsors, and they're often in the tabloids, not the storybooks."

"So you don't believe in romance or fairytales?"

"Those are two different things. Fairytales are fabricated stories."

"And romance?"

Leo looked off in the distance. "Romance is real. But not everyone gets to have it."

"I can't imagine marrying for anything but love. What's the point?"

"Financial security. Protection. Duty. That's why the

nobility married in the past, as well as in the present. A lot of commoners still marry for convenience. Romantic love is only a few hundred years old."

"It's been written about for thousands of years."

"So have fairytales."

"Well then, it's lucky for us that we're both common folk, and we can choose to marry for love and not duty."

"Yes. Lucky us."

A throat cleared behind them. Esme looked up to see the disapproving Giles glaring once more at her.

"My apologies, Esme, but duty calls." There was true regret in Leo's voice. "I have to get back to work. It was lovely meeting you."

He reached out for her hand. She gave it to him. There were pie crumbs on her fingertips. She jerked to bring her hand back in an effort to wipe the pie off, but Leo stayed her hand. He turned her palm over, and he kissed it.

Butterflies went off in Esme's belly. She wanted to say something, but her tongue was tied. And the moment she had her wits about her, he was gone.

CHAPTER FIVE

eo licked his fingers, catching the last crumbs of morsels from the sweet treat that reminded him of home. The golden crust had transported him to the sandy beaches of the island just east of Barcelona. The sweet and fruity notes had called to the French wine country to Cordoba's north. And the spice mixture gave a kick to his Moorish ancestors from the south. The pie maker had captured all of Cordovian history and culture in one perfect bite.

"Can you order a few of these for tonight's dinner?" Leo said to Giles.

Giles pulled out his cell phone and placed the order while Leo licked the last bit from his fingertips. It was bad manners to suckle one's fingers, to be sure, but there was no one watching him. Giles was preoccupied with the pie maker. The driver had his eyes on the road. And Leo's mind was ... elsewhere.

Just up ahead, he saw the dry cleaning truck with the green dragon logo parked at a storefront. Had it been in motion, Leo might have the notion of charging forward into the fray once more. But his damsel was safely ensconced on a stool back in the pie shop.

Leo wondered if he put his ear to Giles's phone if he might hear her tinkling laughter. Catch the slight hitch of her breath as she leaned in and listened to him recite the boring details of his job, a job he'd pretended wasn't his. Yet, she'd been fascinated all the same.

Esme had called him a knight, a hero. As a real king, he was none of those. He was just a nobleman in a suit. A businessman really. And the title placed him as a figurehead with a lot of responsibility. One of those responsibilities was finding a new wife.

He thought of Esme's smile. Their easy banter. Her wild imagination. Her American accent and girl-next-door good looks. She was likely as red-blooded as an American could get. No hint of royal blue was likely to run in her veins.

She was all wrong for him, of course. Definitely not a candidate to sit beside him on the throne. But a delightful lunch companion to sit beside him on a stool.

He'd enjoyed their conversation. He'd enjoyed the escape she'd offered him, even if only for a moment. Over a slice of pie, he'd been a regular Joe chatting up a girl casually. He'd never done anything casual in his life. His every move, thought, and decisions were a matter of state.

His time with Esme had been his escape into an imaginary storybook. Now it was back to business as the car pulled up to the United Nations headquarters.

The tall glass and concrete structure looked like any other office building in the city. One of its distinguishing characteristics was the array of flags flying from posts. There were dozens. One hundred and ninety-three to be exact. Leo easily spotted the Cordovian flag with its staunch orange, red, and blue colors.

"You have your notes?" asked Giles.

Of course, he did. He was always prepared. But Giles had to ask the question, it was his job.

Leo knew that others in Giles's position had a time with their noblemen. Alex couldn't keep a valet or an assistant. The men, and one woman, gave up in a matter of weeks trying to wrangle the man. Most of the times, they couldn't find Alex as he'd often hopped on a jet or yacht and was off in some obscure corner of the globe stuffing his face full of exotic dishes. Leo was the perfect employer and royal. Giles really shouldn't complain.

"What have you done to your suit?" Giles looked down at him in horror. A few smudges from his time in the street with Esme remained at the bottom of his jacket.

"Oh, I rescued a damsel in distress. Esme, the woman from the pie shop." With her name on his tongue, Leo got one last blast of sweetness just behind his two front teeth that he'd somehow missed. He swallowed the final tidbit and felt its presence move to the back of his throat and down his chest.

Giles was not amused. "Here, switch with me."

Leo did. Luckily, he and Giles were the same size, and Giles's coat was nearly as fine as Leo's. With that disaster averted, and the last traces of his adventure gone, they headed into the building.

The UN's role was to maintain international peace and security. Cordoba was under no threat. The small country hadn't been for centuries. Once upon a time, Leo's ancestors had a stronghold in the lands of what would become present day Spain and France. But with a violent history, the people were torn apart, boundaries were shifted over until finally, the present day Cordovians found themselves on a lush island in the Mediterranean.

The people couldn't complain. The island was surrounded by pristine beaches. Inwards were lush valleys and tall mountains. The soil was fertile, and the fish were plenty.

Another part of the UN charter was to protect human rights. Cordoba had no charges of inhumane violations. Even in a country populated by former enemies who'd ransacked each other's ancestors, there was now a harmony amongst the mix of French, Spanish, and African fellows.

When it came to humanitarian aid, thanks to its fishing industry and the oil found surrounding the island, Cordoba was rich enough to help its neighbors. But there was more opportunity to be had. Leo was here to place his hand out for another of the UN's chartered goals; that of sustainable development.

"We are a small island state," he said from his place at the lectern. "We have had great success and prosperity that we'd like to share with you, our international countrymen. Our ancestors braved wars, moved borders, segregated, integrated, and, through it all, we survived and came out the other end stronger. We may be small, but we are mighty."

In his speech, he didn't mention that poverty was on the rise last year, or that teen pregnancy was on an uptick. The older citizens were financially stable and content in established industries. But the young people of Cordoba had few job prospects and too much free time. Those who were bright and ambitious were leaving the country in droves. Those who saw little or no opportunity were procrastinating and procreating.

The government had to create a new industry to keep its youth occupied and remaining in the country. But all Cordovian resources were tapped. He needed fresh blood, fresh blue blood.

At the end of his speech, Leo was greeted with polite applause. He knew he'd succeeded when two individuals approached him. All along, the speech had been for an audience of two.

The Duke of Almodovar was a stout man with a round belly and a curling, gray mustache. The man had used his title to build an empire on seas, much like his pirate ancestors. His was the favor Leo courted. But more importantly, it was the woman who walked beside him whose attention Leo hoped to capture.

"King Leonidas, may I present my daughter, Lady Teresa Nadal, the future duchess of Almodovar."

Lady Teresa curtsied and then extended her hand. Leo took the offered hand, planting a light kiss to Lady Teresa's knuckles. He'd expected a strong whiff of expensive perfumes. He was pleasantly surprised by the smell of sweet cinnamon.

"I was very impressed by your speech," said Lady Teresa. "I wondered if you might find the time on your schedule to talk shop?"

"Please excuse my daughter," said the duke. "The family business is never far from her pretty mind."

What was on the mind of most daughters of nobility was the family business of maintaining the royal line. He'd heard that Lady Teresa had more industrial interests, which suited Leo's needs perfectly.

"I don't mind at all," Leo said. "In fact, I'm having a dinner party tonight. Just a small gathering of the state senator, the mayor, and a few other dignitaries. I would love it if you and your daughter could attend."

"My father has another engagement," said Lady Teresa. "But I would be delighted."

The Almodovars were one of the most successful

maritime construction builders in all of Europe. Cordoba had maximized its use of its land. Now Leo aimed to conquer the waters. He needed a partnership with the family to do so. What better way to build a bridge than the old fashioned way; marriage between nobility.

CHAPTER SIX

The staff of Global Learning Preparatory Academy was in a tizzy when Esme returned thirty minutes later. Outside the building, she'd seen another car with orange, red, and blue flags parked at the front of the school in the school bus zone. Apparently, diplomatic immunity extended to the Kiss and Ride lane.

Esme wondered if Leo was here. But he'd said he and the pinched-face Giles were joining the king at the United Nations Headquarters. This had to be the ride of the princess and the king's younger brother, the prince.

Esme made her way down to her room as the mostly female teachers and staff whispered in each other's ears and giggled behind their hands like middle schoolers. Esme didn't catch sight of the prince. Her mind was elsewhere.

Just this morning, Esme had been excited about the prospect of breathing the same air as a real live prince. But since meeting the royal bodyguard, her temperature and attention had been redirected. Sure, Esme read plenty of fairytales as a kid. But as a grown woman, many of the romance novels on her shelf featured valiant, bare-chested knights who rushed into battle for the unattainable lady promised to the evil prince or aging king.

Leo could definitely fit that bill and then some. But she doubted she'd run into him again. Unless he had another hankering for spicy meat pie. Esme would just have to make sure and make herself available at Jan's until closing today and as much time as she could tomorrow in hopes of another chance encounter with her hunky knight.

She paid no heed to the crowd gathered at the conference room where she was sure the prince and princess were. Unfortunately, the royal pair wouldn't be touring or stopping in her room. Principal Clarke had hand selected Mrs. Truesdale's Stepford children for the class observation. He wouldn't likely let such dignitaries near Esme's unpredictable classroom.

She still wasn't broken into the GLPA way. Esme never intended to be. She was all for striving for academic excellence, but these kids deserved the time and the chance to be, well, kids.

"We've been sleeping," Esme said as the last of her class roused from their nap, "So, you know what that means; time to get our bodies moving. Who's ready for math?"

"Ms. Pickett," said Aubrey after a yawn, "when I learned math last year in pre-kindergarten summer enrichment we did it with pencil and paper."

"I bet you did." Esme put the last of the sleeping mats back into the cubby. "But was it fun?"

The little girl scrunched up her nose as though she didn't understand the meaning of the three letter word.

"Physical education stimulates the brain," Esme said. "We're going to practice our numbers while moving our bodies to get our whole person involved in the lesson."

This explanation passed the girl's smell test, and Aubrey nodded in approval.

"All right class, the number of the day is five. If I say or show you a number greater than five, you will stand up. If I say or show you a number less than five, you will sit down. Who's ready?"

There was a loud chorus of *meeeees*.

"Four," Esme called out. The entire class sat down.

She held up a sign with the number seven on it. Everyone stood back up.

"Three plus four," Esme said.

Aubrey and Tracey stayed standing. A few other kids wobbled. Carla Barrow sat down. The stragglers looked between Aubrey and Carla and remained standing.

"Hold up three fingers on one hand," Esme said to Carla. The little girl did as she was instructed. "Now hold up four fingers on the other hand."

"Neither is bigger than five," Carla announced triumphantly.

"True, but I said plus. Count all of your fingers."

Carla did. When she got to the fingers on the second hand, her lips began to quiver. "I got it wrong?"

"Yes, you did sweetheart. But now you'll know better for the next time. You just learned a lesson, and that's what school is all about."

Carla opened her eyes wide. Instead of the light of understanding Esme was hoping for, her tear ducts opened and spilled. A sorrowful moan escaped her lips.

Esme took a deep breath. As a compassionate person, she wanted to console the girl. But at the same time, she knew there was another lesson to be had in not always being right, not always winning, not having everyone receive a medal for participation.

"Not everyone wins. I don't expect you to be perfect. I expect you to do your best. If you always do your best, even if you don't get it right, you'll always make someone proud, especially me."

It was the perfect Hallmark moment. Carla's tears dried up, but there was still no aha moment. "I'm sure that's wrong, Ms. Pickett."

Esme sighed.

This was the generation where all children must receive birthday invites. On Valentine's Day, parents were instructed to send cards to every kid in the class. These kids would know nothing of rejection or unrequited love. They would believe everyone they met would accept and love them equally.

They were all doomed.

"Actually, my father says the same thing to me. He's a king, so I'm certain it's right."

They all turned to the door. What could only be described as a miniature fairy stood in the doorway. She was dressed in pale blue with patent leather shoes. She looked like she was ready for Easter on a fall day. Dark hair was tied into a perfect bun atop her oval-shaped head. There was lace on her dress that looked finer than anything Esme owned, and she wore a white cardigan overtop the ensemble. Bold choice for a five-year-old.

A number of adults stood behind her. One of them was the principal looking green beneath the gills as he peered into Esme's room. The other adult was a dark haired man with a devastating grin and sparkling hazel eyes that were hauntingly familiar.

"Are you the princess?" asked Kurt.

"She can't be the princess," said Aubrey. "She's not wearing a crown."

"And she doesn't have a sword to fight a dragon," said Tracey.

"Anyone can wear a crown," said the princess. "It's your family that makes you noble."

"Wow," sighed Esme. "That is so profound."

The little girl's hazel eyes found hers. Once again, Esme couldn't shake the feeling that she was looking into a familiar face. "My father said that, too."

"He must be a wise king," said Esme.

The little princess nodded.

"Thank God he's not here to hear you say that," said the man behind her who Esme assumed was the prince. "It would make his huge head even huger."

"Uncle Alex, there's no such word as huger, and father's head is entirely proportionate."

"All right, Penelope," said the prince, "it's time to go. We have to get to class. I can't believe I just said that."

Prince Alex grimaced as though truly pained. He was quite handsome. Esme waited for her belly to grow butterflies. She was surprised to learn it didn't.

"So sorry to have disturbed you," said the prince.

His hazel eyes connected with hers, and she felt a flutter. But not for him. For the color. They were the same color as Leo's. Esme wondered if all Cordovians had the same gold flecks in their brown eyes?

"No trouble at all," she said after she realized she'd been staring.

"Can't I visit this class?" asked Princess Penelope.

Behind her, the principal's eyes went large, huger than saucers.

Esme stepped forward to save the man from his perfectly planned itinerary for the royals, which would lead them far away from her uncommon class. "Well, sweetie—"

The principal coughed. Esme looked up, unsure what was wrong now? Then she realized her folly.

"I mean, your highness, the other class worked very hard preparing for your visit. You wouldn't want to disappoint them, would you?"

"You're very diplomatic," said Princess Penelope.

"You know some very big words for a five-year-old."

"I'm nearly six."

"Ah, now I see. That explains it."

The little princess grinned, looking like a child for the first time since she'd stepped up to the threshold of the classroom. "As you said, not everyone wins."

Esme cringed. That was not an edict that the school liked to put forth even though it was the truth.

"But," Princess Penelope continued, "if I were trying to do what's best for everyone, I could invite the other class to yours."

"Now, look who's being diplomatic."

"It's what I'm going to be when I grow up."

"A diplomat?"

"I thought she was going to be a dragon slayer?" Kurt whispered behind Esme as quietly as a five-year-old could, which was at full volume.

"May I try your game?" asked the princess.

Such pretty manners. Esme looked up to the prince. He shrugged but was smiling. She looked to Principal Clarke. His shoulders were tense. She was sure she'd get an earful for this display after the school bell rang.

"I've never seen learning like that," said the princess. "My tutors just use pencil and paper."

"Me too," said Aubrey. "But Ms. Pickett can be weird sometimes. Fun weird but still weird."

And so, with Principal Clarke standing guard, Princess

Penelope came into Esme's classroom for a rousing lesson of math movements where she got each and every question right. By the end of the lesson, she wore a huge grin on her pretty face and was somewhat out of breath from all the brain and physical activity.

"That was fun," she said to Esme, hazel eyes twinkling like stars were hidden in their depths.

"I'm glad you enjoyed it," said Esme.

"All right, little pea, it's time to go," said Prince Alex from his station at the wall where he'd promptly pulled out and engaged his cell phone for the ten-minute lesson.

"I'd like to see you again," Princess Penelope said to Esme. "Perhaps we can discuss fractions over dinner?"

"Math at dinner?" asked Esme.

"She's a strange child," said the prince. "She actually enjoys school. Meanwhile, I'm getting hives being this close to chalk."

Esme laughed. She didn't giggle. The prince was charming as a prince should be. But during their entire encounter, he hadn't once sent her heart aflutter like a certain knight in his employ.

"My father is having a dinner party tonight," said Princess Penelope. "I'm sure I can invite a guest."

Principal Clarke grit his teeth. But this wasn't his territory. Esme was being asked to dine with royals. Which meant she might get to see Leo again. And besides, who wouldn't want to have dinner with a princess, even if it was to discuss fractions.

CHAPTER SEVEN

"*I* am so glad you could come tonight, Senator."

Leo shook the dozenth hand that night. His jaw ached from being stretched wide into a grin for hours that morning after his speech. Then his jovial grin and pumping of hands continued on into the afternoon as he hobnobbed with the world's most powerful movers and shakers. He'd barely gotten a moment's rest before opening his own doors to receive more guests.

That was the job. He was the chief spokesperson for Cordoba. The guests he welcomed and schmoozed tonight would help keep Cordoba's future bright and profitable.

Cordoba had many trade agreements with western countries hungry for oil. The waters around the island had a few reserves that, even after decades of pumping, still showed no sign of running dry. The spices culled from their cumin farms were always in high demand. The fine silk textiles they produced had recently come back in fashion and were presently being walked down high fashion runways.

U.S. Senators, British Parliamentary members, and

French officials weren't the only high-powered players at tonight's dinner. There were also a few socialites strategically seated around the table. The strategy had not been Leo's doing, it had been the women's own.

Alan Atwood was a titan of the hotel industry, and Leo was happy to speak with him about the possibilities of developing a resort off the Cordovian coastline. Atwood hadn't been on the original guest list. He was likely there at the bequest of his social climbing daughter, Alana.

Luckily, Alana Atwood wasn't interested in Leo. She had her sights set on Alex. But to have Alex tell it, he'd been there, done that, and gotten the polyester-blend t-shirt.

Hosting is where Leo shined. He was a people person through and through just like his own father. He was able to suss out the needs of those around him and fill them. Unlike his brother who was content to escape to dark corners of the world to try out exotic cuisine while hitting on anything in a skirt. So long as they didn't ask for a ring, Alex was happy to spend his money on jewelry and fine dining for his victims.

Leo found his brother in the kitchen area of the hotel suite, likely hiding out from the hotel huntress.

"Where did you get this pie?" Alex said around a full mouth of bisteeva. "Did you fly it in from home?"

"That was for dessert," Leo admonished.

"You know I always have my dessert first."

"There's a pie shop in the city. It's near the school you and Pen visited today. How was that, by the way?"

"Very well. She learned math by standing and sitting, it was quite rousing. And she invited the teacher over for dinner."

"What?" Leo's mouth fell open.

"To discuss fractions or something."

"You let Penelope invite a stranger into our home?"

"This isn't our home." Alex waved his fork around the room. "It's a hotel. And you know Giles had vetted everyone at the school before we even stepped out of the car."

Leo looked to the back entry way to the kitchen which led to the sleeping quarters. Down the hall, his daughter, who had been offered the chance to see a Broadway play and declined, was entertaining a teacher and the joys of parts of a whole.

"What was this teacher like? Did she seem the social climbing type like our hotel heiress out there?"

Alex looked back into the dining area and cringed. "No, nothing of the sort. I mean she was attractive. That all-American kind of cute. You know, girl-next-door."

Leo saw where this was going. Alex had likely invited this woman over because he was hot for teacher as the song went. "If you invited this woman over for a fling, just don't make out in front of my child. Get another room, will you."

"She's not my type. Too many brains in her head."

"Great. Then you can spend the evening entertaining our guests."

"You mean meet my new sister." Alex poked his head around the corner as Lady Teresa came in. "She's quite the looker. I hear she's smart, accomplished, good breeding record, and royal blue blood. She's perfect for you."

"Yes." Leo nodded as he watched Teresa take off her coat to reveal a perfectly proportioned figure below her brilliant mind. "She's perfect."

"Well, don't make out with her in front of my niece or anything."

Leo gave his brother a playful shove. They both entered the dining room as the servers placed the food on the table, and the meal began in earnest. With his other business dealings done, Leo sat next to Lady Teresa. She wore the same cinnamon scent as earlier. Her blue eyes held his, showing genuine interest, as he spoke.

"I went to school in the states," she said. "Harvard."

"Oxford," said Leo. "I understand you like water sports?"

"Nearly made the Women's Olympic Team in sailing. I understand you're a pretty good fencer?"

"Not good enough to make the Olympic Team."

Her head tilted back ever so slightly, and she laughed. She hadn't thrown her head back and giggled. She placed her hand lightly at her chest and didn't give him a whack on the shoulder. No, she was well raised in the proper decorum of a royal woman.

"We have a lot in common," Lady Teresa said. "We're both blue bloods. Our family businesses could benefit the other for industrial purposes. You know what that means?"

It would be the height of ill-breeding for Leo's mouth to hang open. Which is what his jaw nearly did. But because he was well trained, he clamped his mouth shut and smiled politely.

"It means wedding bells," she continued.

Leo's jaw wrenched open, and a series of choking sounds escaped. He reached for his glass and took a sip to help recover.

"Forgive me," said Lady Teresa. "I'm pretty blunt."

"No, I appreciate that." Leo sat his drained glass back on the table.

"Let's make a pact to be honest with each other," she said. "I'm an old crow by nobility standards. I've sown my oats, as I'm sure you did before your first marriage."

Leo chose to say nothing. Certainly not that his wife had been his first and only lover.

"I've had great accomplishments on my own. I still have goals to meet. I know the value of a good partner in business. I can see the value of a partner in life. A girl can't do better than a king."

"I thought all little girls dreamed of princes."

"I'm a grown woman," said Teresa. "Being of noble blood, I didn't grow up believing in fairytales. In fact, my mother banned the books from the castle so that I would only ever imagine my true duties."

Isabel had done the same when Penelope was born. She'd said she wanted her children to be realistic about royalty. Not have fanciful dreams that the law and tradition would not allow.

"I grew up in a castle with no dragons or witches," Lady Teresa continued. "I did have two evil stepmothers after my parents' divorce. But," and here she paused for emphasis, "I don't believe in divorce. Once you make a merger, you stick with it and make it work."

On that, Leo agreed. There had never been a divorce in Cordovian royalty. Infidelity, suspected murder, sure. But not a single divorce decree in all the country's ancient history.

"True love isn't afforded people like us," Teresa was saying. "As I said, I've learned to make good partnerships in business. I believe those skills will translate nicely to marriage. I say we have a few more meetings about our families' needs, we can call a few of them dates, and see if we can't come to a lifelong agreement."

It was exactly what Leo knew was the right thing. It was likely how his parents had arranged his first marriage. So, what was holding him back from sealing this deal right on the spot?

Leo looked up and saw a flash of ... something. Or someone. He thought he'd seen someone standing in the entry hall way, but all of his guests had arrived. In another blink of an eye, the flash was gone.

"This weekend is Cordoba's Union Day?"

"Yes," said Leo, coming back to the conversation that could unite the generations in his country. "Why don't you plan a visit to Cordoba to see the festivities?"

"Sounds lovely."

They sat for a moment, both grinning politely at each other. Suddenly, Leo's jaw felt tired. He needed a moment to relax it. "Would you excuse me? I'm going to go check on my daughter and say good night."

CHAPTER EIGHT

oming into the Waldorf Astoria, the same hotel where a maid played by Jennifer Lopez ran into a billionaire played by Ralph Fiennes in *Maid in Manhattan*, the same hotel where Al Pacino sniffed out love in *Scent of a Woman*, the same hotel where Eddie Murphy came to America, Esme realized something. She was woefully underdressed.

She'd worn the very best dress she had. It was a step above a cocktail dress hanging below her knees and brushing her ankles. But it was a step below prom dress with a plunging neckline. Only because she'd had it altered after she'd worn it to prom for a college cocktail party. And then again, for a teacher's union gala.

The neckline dropped a bit more with each alteration. Plunging might be the wrong word, but the casual onlooker definitely got the message that she was working with a little something-something on her chest. Not that she was actually working with much.

The dress was princess cut with long seams that stitched together to fit her form. It was a deep garnet color. That deep red had always made Esme think of royalty over the traditional blue or purple. Maybe because it was the color of blood and the path to royalty always came with bloodshed. At least in the history books, maybe not the storybooks.

She'd worn her best jewelry. It was mostly of the costume variety, but the necklace she wore was real. That was because there was only one jewel. A garnet the same color as her dress. It was her most expensive look. And it was not enough.

She'd come into the hotel behind a woman dressed in a gown straight out of *Cosmopolitan*. It was clear her jewels were real. She didn't smell of floral soap; she smelled of cinnamon. Likely an expensive perfume that wasn't over the counter. It was probably mixed especially for her.

The woman had been allowed entry into the elevator that went up to the penthouse where the royals of Cordoba were staying. Esme had been held back instead of heading directly up to the royal suite. The concierge had checked her credentials twice. Then dialed up to the royal suite and had a long conversation with someone on the other end of the line. Ten minutes later, finally, she was allowed up.

When the elevator hit the top floor, Esme's belly was in knots. Likely from the altitude. When the doors opened, her belly dropped.

She'd been hoping to find Leo on the other side, guarding the royals within. She'd given her name and hoped he'd remembered and would be there on the other side of the doors to greet her. Instead, she found his friend Giles. Giles did not look happy to see her.

"Hi," Esme waved. "Remember me from the pie shop? Well, after the pie shop, I met the princess and—"

But Giles had already turned on his heel during her verbal diarrhea. "The staff has finished serving dinner."

"Oh. Am I late?"

Giles turned, finally looking at her. The look he gave her said he thought she was addled in the brain. "You'll keep to the kitchen area. Your lesson will be only an hour. The princess has a strict schedule to keep."

"A five-year-old has a strict schedule?"

"Bed time."

"Oh. Of course. It's just, I thought we were having dinner?"

He turned again, with a sneer this time. "From what I understand, you're here to teach fractions to Princess Penelope. Nothing more."

"Right. Of course."

They passed by the dining room, but the door was only open a crack so Esme couldn't see into it. Esme could hear the chatter and clink of wine glasses. The smell of expensive food wafted out. She hadn't eaten in anticipation of a few courses. Her stomach grumbled.

Giles turned back to her. His gaze fell down to her belly as though the singular organ had offended him.

"Sorry," said Esme.

With a final turn on his heel, he led her into the kitchen. It was already cleaned and cleared of dishes. Esme chided herself. She'd actually thought she'd gotten invited to dine with royalty.

But all was not lost. Leo might be around one of these corners. She still might get a chance to see him before her hour was up, and she had to return to the ground floor.

"Hello, Ms. Pickett."

"Hello, Penelope."

"You are to address the princess as your royal highness," said Giles. "And curtsey."

"Oh. I'm sorry, your royal highness." Esme bent both her

knees, but that didn't work. She put one foot behind the other but nearly tripped over the hem of her dress.

Princess Penelope bit her lip. And then a giggle escaped.

Giles turned and glared at Esme. "You are to keep to this room. His majesty, the King, has important guests tonight."

"Yes, Giles," said Princess Penelope. "I know. Thank you."

The man straightened, not taking his eyes off Esme until the last moment. He bowed to the little girl. And left the room.

"Now that is some super power," said Esme. "Being able to dismiss a curmudgeon like that."

"Giles isn't so bad. He plays chess with me when we're back home. Everyone's just very protective of me. They have been since my mother died."

"I'm so sorry," said Esme. "I didn't know that. I lost my mother when I was just a girl, too. I was just a few years older than you."

"I can barely remember her."

"My mother used to read me a lot of stories. She left me all of her storybooks. When I read them, I remember her."

"I wish I had memories like that."

"Your father doesn't like to talk about her?"

"He doesn't mind. He just doesn't have any memories that help. All of his memories I can find in the royal archives; their wedding, their coronation; their official duties. But nothing personal like reading to me in bed."

Esme's heart ached for the little girl. But Penelope's shoulders remained straight, her back erect, her dainty hands crossed in front of her.

"Anyway," she said, "I'd much rather talk about fractions. I've brought out my books. I love math."

Esme looked at the textbooks gathered. She'd never met

a five-year-old who'd said those words. And she worked with gifted students.

Textbooks were not Esme's jam. Even in college, she felt that the best learning was done by experiencing the world. She looked around at the kitchen for inspiration.

"How about we learn fractions in a practical way?" said Esme.

"Oh, yes," Penelope grinned. "Do you have a game? Perhaps nothing too physical in this small space."

The small space was bigger than Esme's entire apartment. "I have something better than sitting and standing. Baking."

Of course, the pantry of a suite for royals was stocked to the brim. In a matter of minutes, Esme found everything she needed and piled the materials on the counter.

"We are going to make cookies," said Esme. "We need to start with one cup of butter."

"But this is a stick." Penelope held up the long, yellow rectangle.

"Exactly. And it measures in tablespoons. So, how many tablespoons will it take to fill up this measuring cup?"

Princess Penelope's eyes widened in wonder. She took the cup and a butter knife and began to slice off pats of butter until she got to sixteen. "Sixteen tablespoons is the same as one cup."

"You got it. Now let's do the sugar." Esme paused. "Are you allowed to have sugar?"

"Of course."

Esme breathed a sigh of relief. They measured the tablespoons of sugar, the teaspoons of baking powder and soda. They nearly had all the ingredients measured and prepared.

"I'm having trouble with the flour," said Esme tugging at

the corners of the unopened bag. And of course, the bag exploded as she gave it another tug. The white powder spilled all over both Princess Penelope's and Esme's dresses. "Oh, no."

But the princess only giggled. "Don't worry. One of the maids will clean it up."

"Oh no, missy. We made this mess. We need to clean it up."

Princess Penelope stared at her with wide eyes. Obviously, Esme had messed up protocol again.

Esme tried the curtsey again. "We need to clean this up, your royal highness."

The frown dissolved and another set of giggles erupted from the little girl. "I've never had to clean up my own mess. This will be another lesson. I'll find the broom. I think I know where it's kept."

The little girl dashed around the corner, grinning from ear to ear. Esme was now the one left gaping. Normally, she had to invent a game to get her kindergartners to clean up. But the promise of a new skill was all it took for this little lady.

Esme turned back to the ingredients assembled. In the doorway, there stood a figure. She braced herself for another of Giles's disapproving scowls that not only had she made a mess, but enlisted her royal highness' help in cleaning it up.

But it wasn't Giles standing and staring at her in the doorway.

"Hi, Leo."

"What are you doing here?" he said, his hazel eyes huger than when he'd rescued her from a dry cleaning dragon.

"Princess Penelope invited me. She came to my class this afternoon."

"You're the kindergarten teacher?"

Esme nodded. "I was hoping to bump into you while I was here."

"You were?"

"Hello, father." Penelope came back around the corner with a broom and dust pan in her hands.

Esme's eyes went between the dark-haired girl with the bright hazel eyes and her ... father.

CHAPTER NINE

This was not a fairytale, Leo told the synapses firing in his brain. It was a mess. It was a pretty mess because the fireworks that ignited as his neurotransmitters made and received connections looked remarkably like the sparkles that would come out of a Disney character's magic wand. They translated the scene before him of a messy cooking experiment into a Cinderella-themed spectacle.

Esme stood in the kitchen of his hotel suite. She wore a dress the color of a ripe apple. It hugged each and every one of her curves rousing Leo's imagination further. The bodice pushed up her breasts which heaved as she laughed with Penelope.

Esme had been transformed from the attractive young woman in common working clothes that he'd encountered that afternoon, to a dazzling damsel in a regal gown who had snuck into the ball against her evil stepmother's wishes. Even with the flour coating her gown, she was breathtaking. Leo's palms itched to present her with a shoe that was just her size.

The way she looked at him, he could tell she would happily slip her bare foot into the slipper that was only meant for her. But looking down, he saw that her feet weren't bare. She wore sensible shoes, and he didn't have a pair that he could give her.

Finally, Leo's gaze shifted down to his daughter. The grin on Penelope's face took him aback. His daughter was always so serious, even as a baby. Her mother had been the same. So had Leo's mother. He couldn't remember any of the women in his life ever giggling.

Had Leo ever made Penelope giggle? He'd certainly made her smile. But had he ever made his little girl laugh uncontrollably such that her little shoulders shook with the effort. Penelope's eyes lit up when she saw him, and then she announced who he truly was.

"Father?" Esme asked. "As in … the king?"

In an instant, her view of him changed. Her bright, welcoming eyes clouded with surprise, then dismay, then confusion. He would've given anything to go back to Regular Joe Leo in her eyes. But that man had been his own fairytale. King Leonidas lived in the real world high in the sky in castles and luxury hotel penthouses where girls next door had no access.

But here she was.

What was she doing here?

"You're the kindergarten teacher?" he asked.

Esme nodded. She didn't hold his gaze any longer. Her hands fidgeted. Smoothing her gown, her fingers streaked the fabric white with flour.

Leo took great comfort in that small act of anxiety. Esme had liked him when she thought he simply worked for the crown. Now that she knew he *was* the crown, she took a step back. Most women were only interested in that bit of jewelry on his head. It made him want to come near to her.

"We made a mess," Penelope was saying. "But Ms. Pickett insists we clean it up. You always say we must heed the culture of our host, so I'm doing it her way."

"That's very diplomatic of you, Pea," said Leo.

"Pea?" The smile was back on Esme's face. "Like The Princess and the Pea?"

"No," said Penelope. "It's short for Penelope. Only father and Uncle Alex call me that. You may call me it as well. If you like?"

"I'd like that. Thank you, Pea."

Esme smiled warmly down at Penelope. His daughter's eyes practically twinkled under Esme's shining gaze. Leo knew he had to shake himself out of it. He knew that eyes couldn't twinkle, not really. So, why did he feel a tiny sizzle on his skin when Esme directed her sparkling gaze back at him?

"Ms. Pickett is an excellent tutor," said Penelope. "She turned fractions into a treat. I imagine I may get a lesson out of cleaning up as well."

Penelope ran the broom over the white powder on the floor. Her light brushes and directionless sweeps only served to make more of a mess. Leo stepped up to take the broom from his daughter.

"Here, darling," he said. "I'll help."

"Oh, no," Esme grabbed for the broom at the same time. "This is my fault ... erm, your highness."

"He's your majesty," said Penelope.

"Ms. Pickett has my permission to call me by my Christian name," Leo said.

Esme shook her head. "I couldn't. I can't."

They both still had their hands on the broom handle.

She gave a tug. He didn't relent. She sighed and released her grip, but when she took a step back, it was right into the patch of flour, and she wobbled backward.

Leo sprang into action. Releasing the broom with a clatter, he caught her in his arms. For the second time today, he held this woman in his embrace.

Because it was an embrace. It had stopped being a rescue the moment he knew she'd regained her balance and her feet were sturdy beneath her. It had stopped being a rescue when his hold tightened even though she was no longer in danger of falling. It had stopped being a rescue when he realized he was perfectly content to remain this way for the rest of his night, and if he were honest, much, much longer.

Warmth spread through Leo as he continued the embrace. He felt a tingling up his spine. His eyes latched onto hers like they were magnets. Her palms came to rest on his chest. Even through the layers of fine fabric, her touch scorched him, as though her fingertips placed an invisible brand just to the right of his heart.

Esme looked down at his chest where her hands lay, and her eyes widened. "Oh, no. I've made a mess of your clothes again."

Leo looked down at his dinner jacket. The brand was there, emblazoned in stark white against his dark jacket. He slowly released his hold on her, making sure that she was, in fact, steady on her own two feet. A pang of disappointment swept through him that she didn't wobble when he left her to her own reconnaissance.

"I am so sorry, your highness. I mean, your majesty." She lifted her hands and brushed at his coat. Due to the fact that her hands were still covered in flour, all she did was make the matter worse.

Leo did not stop her.

"I'm making things worse, aren't I?"

She was.

The longer she stood near him, the more details he catalogued of her face. She had a smattering of light freckles across her nose. Her eyes weren't uniformly brown, there were a few light flecks at the edge that reminded him of a Tiger's Eye stone. And then there was that delectable, sweet scent he'd gotten a taste of that morning.

His neurotransmitters worked over time capturing the fine print of Esmeralda Pickett. The details imprinted on him. He knew this singular moment would be catalogued amongst one of the memories that would flash before his eyes on his death bed, right up there with his coronation and the birth of his daughter, as one of the pivotal moments of his life.

By the look in her eyes, he wondered if she was thinking the same? Was her brain cataloguing this moment between them? Would she remember it for all time?

"Look, father," said Penelope. "We're using fractions to make cookies."

That was enough to break the spell. Leo turned from Esme to his daughter. "That sounds like a good use of math. Don't let me stop you."

"Yes, what's next, Ms. Pickett?" Penelope stepped over the broom and the flour. She pushed aside the mess and focused on the mini bowl.

Esme looked down at the mess.

"Don't worry," said Leo. "I'll have the staff tend to this. It appears to me that the three of us will only serve to make the mess bigger. Let's finish the lesson instead."

Esme measured out flour and tossed it into the bowl. "All right, Princess Pea, why don't you mix the dough."

Penelope's grin was huge as she took the wooden spoon and began to stir.

Esme bent down to pick up the bag of flour. She walked around the counter to where Leo stood, careful to step over the pile of flour still on the floor. She lifted her dress and pressed the foot handle on the trash bin.

"Why didn't you tell me you were a king?" Her voice was quiet, only loud enough for him to hear.

"Why didn't you tell me you were a school teacher?"

The bin closed with a thud. She looked up at him, wrinkling her nose as though confused.

"At the moment," he said, "neither of our occupations made a difference."

She raised her finger the way his old school teachers used to when they found fault with his answers. "You didn't go on about the state of education in the world or teachers today being inadequate."

"I don't feel that way at all about education."

She huffed, balling her fingers into a fist. "I went on and on about princes and fairytales."

"Showing your own prejudices against all other royals aside from princes and displaying your stereotypical views on dragons."

She gave him a blank stare that showed him she wasn't amused. Only problem was the grin warring at the corner of her mouth. "And you're continuing to laugh at my expense."

"Not at all," Leo grinned. "A little imagination is good. You simply have a lot."

She narrowed her gaze. Her hand unballed and that finger rose again, ready to make a counter point.

"The dough is mixed," Penelope announced. "Can we bake them?"

Leo looked up at the clock. He'd been away from his guests longer than he'd planned. "It's your bedtime."

The joy on Penelope's face fell like a crashing stone.

"We haven't cleaned up our mess," said Esme. "If we put them in the oven now, by the time we finish cleaning, the cookies will be done."

"We do have staff who can—"

She cut him off with another look that he'd seen countless times on his school teachers' and college professors' faces that said he got the answer wrong. They must have a class on that at teachers' school.

"I'm not leaving a mess behind." She glanced down at the powder prints on his coat. "Not any more of a mess. Penelope, you can spoon out one tablespoon of the dough and space them an inch apart on the tray while I sweep."

Leo picked up a rag and began wiping down the counter. Esme paused in her sweeping but didn't say anything. Leo felt as though he'd aced a pop quiz.

By the time he was done with the counter, Penelope had measured and placed all the dough. He helped her put them in the oven and then set the timer for eight minutes. He turned and found Esme watching the two of them with a smile on her face.

"I take it the two of you don't cook often?" she asked.

"I couldn't find my way around a kitchen," he said. "My brother, on the other hand, is a different story."

"Uncle Alex makes the best treats," said Penelope. "I never thought to join him in the kitchen. I'm surprised he's such a good cook. He hates math."

Penelope turned her attention back to the baking cookies. Leo turned his attention back to the kindergarten teacher. She stepped once more on the foot handle of the trash, chucking in the swept flour. Knowing their time was almost up, he took a moment to add a few more details to the memory of her.

She was across the room, but her sweetness overwhelmed him. Or was that the cookies baking in the oven? He wanted to go to her, inhale her, and see for himself. He wanted a few more minutes with her, in this story world he found himself in whenever she was around.

The oven bell dinged.

"They're ready." Penelope clapped her hands.

Leo knew enough to don an oven mitt before retrieving the tray. Once the baking sheet was on the counter, Penelope immediately reached for one of the golden brown treats.

"No, darling."

"No, sweetie."

Both Leo and Esme reached out to stay Penelope's hand at the same time, and their fingers wound up colliding into each other's. Esme took her hand back. But he didn't miss the shudder that went through her shoulders. It thrilled him that he was having an effect on her because he had shuddered too.

"They need time to cool," said Esme. "And you need to wash your hands and put away the dust pan. Not in that order."

Penelope did as she was told.

"I should probably get going," said Esme. "I was told I only had an hour audience with her highness, and I'm sure my pumpkin's coming soon."

"Don't you want to taste the fruits of your labor?" said Leo.

"I already did," Esme tilted her head, looking around him at Penelope washing her hands in the sink. "The sparkle that goes off in a kid's eyes when they learn something new or get a concept that eluded them; that's my currency. Lame, huh?"

"I find it remarkable," he said.

Esme tore her gaze from Penelope to look up at him. There it was again, the sparkle in her eyes. He hadn't imagined it. It was very real.

"Your majesty, what are you doing!"

CHAPTER TEN

*E*sme was caught in Leo's eyes. Correction, King Leo's eyes. He was gazing down at her like something from a storybook. Just the simple brush of his fingers had sent shivers down her spine, just like she'd read about. Holy elves, was she falling in love? Was she living her own real live storybook romance and with a King, no doubt?

He'd come to her rescue not one, but two times all in one day. Sure the last rescue was flour induced. But heck, they counted. Kitchen disasters were the true danger of the twenty-first century woman. Just ask Gretel.

There was definitely something there. She was fooling herself to think otherwise. There was an attraction. One he clearly hadn't been expecting, but she could tell he felt it too by the lingering looks, by the tingle she knew they both experienced, by the way he caught his breath when he'd held her close.

They had a thing.

She knew the signs. She read enough hardback storybooks and watched enough British dramas to know when she saw the signs, there was a thing. And these were clearly blaring signs of thingness.

So, of course, now would be the perfect time for the villain to make an entrance.

Giles looked positively horrified at the sight in the kitchen. They'd done a pretty good job getting the flour up, though she was certain the cleaning staff wouldn't think so. But for two royals who had probably never lifted a finger much less a broom or cleaning rag a day in their lives, they'd done a pretty fair job.

Giles wasn't looking at the white streaks on the counter or floor. He was glaring at Esme.

If she hadn't just been in Leo's arms, if she hadn't just been caught up in his gaze, if she hadn't been counting the various signs of the thing, she would've felt like an insignificant speck under his narrowed gaze. But as it was, Esme was walking on a cloud, and she was not about to come down by ... whoever Giles was to Leo. Not his brother, perhaps a valet? That was still a thing, right?

Giles's razor sharp gaze cut from Esme to Leo. It did not soften. The man must not understand the word job security. "Your guests are waiting, your majesty."

"Oh, no," said Esme, taking a step down from her cloud of happiness. "Leo, I've kept you from your party. And I've messed you up."

She dusted at his jacket, but only wound up smearing more of the flour on his dark suit. Leo didn't stop her. She felt the sparkles going off with each brush of her hand on his person. By the widening of his gaze, she knew he felt it too.

A sharp intake of breath broke their connection.

"I'll handle it," Giles came between them. "I believe this tutoring session is over."

"But the cookies," said Penelope.

"Cookies before bedtime?" frowned Giles. The man couldn't be much older than Leo, but he looked like a grandpa telling the three of them to get off his lawn while handing out toothpaste at Halloween.

"Giles, you do know that we are the King and princess of your home country?"

Giles only raised an eyebrow and held out his hand for Leo's jacket. Leo sighed and shrugged off the ruined garment. Giles looked down at the flour prints with utter dismay. When his gaze lifted, he gave Esme the full side eye.

"I have an idea." Esme raised her hand as though she were the new kid in class. In a way, she was new to the trappings of royal life. "How about one last lesson in fractions? Your highness, if we took one cookie and split it evenly so that we all received a piece, what fraction would that be?"

"One third," Penelope said after some thinking. "Because Giles doesn't have a sweet tooth."

Leo didn't try to hide his grin. Giles was at the sink dabbing at the jacket with wet paper towels.

Penelope used a butter knife to expertly and exactly slice one cookie into three equal pieces. She handed the pieces to Esme and her father and then popped the third piece into her mouth and sighed.

"You can have more tomorrow," said Leo.

"What about Ms. Pickett?" said Penelope.

"No worries," said Esme. "They're for you. You did all the work."

"Now it is your bed time, little pea," said Leo. "Go wash up and hop under the covers."

Penelope gave her father a hug. "Can we do this again? Practice fractions with baking?"

"Of course," said Leo pulling the girl in for a tighter hug.

"I'm sure Uncle Alex will join us," said Penelope. "Maybe we can invite Ms. Pickett again?"

Leo swallowed before looking up. Esme's heart flipped under his perusal. But the light that had burned bright in his eyes every time he gazed at her had dimmed.

"I wish that were possible," he said. "But we leave tomorrow night."

Esme's lips parted. She inhaled, but her chest felt tight. Her stomach clenched and not from want of food.

"Maybe you can come to Cordoba for a visit one day?" Penelope said to her. "This weekend is our annual Union Day Celebration. There will be lots of baking and pastries. There's even a pie making contest."

"Ms. Pickett has a day job, your highness." The way Giles said her last name evoked memories of Principal Clark.

"Thank you for the invitation," Esme said to Penelope. Then her gaze went to Leo. "Maybe one day?"

He didn't respond. He didn't look at her. In fact, he swallowed again.

Oh, no. Had she read the signs wrong? Were they at the end of the story? It wasn't possible? Only happy should come after this, and the mood had decidedly turned somber.

"Your guests, your majesty." Giles handed Leo's dinner jacket back to him. It was pristine as though it had just come from the dry cleaners. All trace of Esme's hand prints gone.

Leo slipped into his coat. "I'm going to walk my daughter's guest out first."

He kissed Penelope goodnight as she made her way out of the kitchen. The little princess offered a smile and a wave to Esme before disappearing down the corridor. Leo turned to Esme and held out his hand indicating that she should precede him.

They walked in silence, passing by the dining room on their way to the front door. The door was wide open now. A few of the guests, dressed in finery, looked up at them as they passed. Frowns skimmed across the dignified diners' faces.

Esme still had flour on her gown, and her hair had come loose. But she had something they didn't have. For one more moment at least, she had the king's attention.

"Thank you for tonight," said Leo. "For what you did with Penelope."

"It was my pleasure."

He looked down at her as though unsure what to do with her now. Leo shifted as though at a loss for words. "I really enjoyed meeting you."

"It was a dream come true for me."

His grin came back, but there was sadness at the corner of his mouth. "Disappointed?"

"That you're not a prince? Yeah, that part's still a bummer."

The sadness shook loose, and he laughed. He was her Leo again. The man she met in the street. The man who'd held her in his embrace long seconds after she'd regained her footing.

"But you did slay a dragon for me," she continued. "And battled flour fairies."

"Flour fairies?"

"Not many girls can say that."

"No girl could say that. Seeing as neither dragons nor fairies are real."

"Must you dash all of my dreams?" Esme sighed dramatically.

"Well, you did dash my coat with flour."

"Can't you just pretend it's fairy dust?"

The sadness crept back into his hazel gaze. "I can't."

Esme felt a shift in him. As though he were changing from Leo to King. This was it. Her fairytale was coming to an end. She'd read her fair share of modern day fairytales. There had even been a few royal romances in reality.

But why did she feel that that sparkling, magical light was now dimming on her? The storybook was closing, shutting her out with no happy ending. There was nothing she could do.

"Well, then." She took a deep breath and let it out. But she had no more stalling tactics. Midnight had struck and left her coated in flour. "Good night, your majesty."

And then his gaze shifted again. "It's Leo."

And it was. Just for one more second. It was a second Esme would hold on to for the rest of her life. That moment she gazed into the eyes of a king and felt the possibility.

"Farewell, Leo."

"Farewell, Esmeralda."

CHAPTER ELEVEN

He'd never had such a crispy cookie that was also moist and chewy at the same time. It was such a sweet contradiction. Leo urged himself to eat slowly, to savor each morsel. Once this was gone, that would be it.

There were more cookies to be sure. A full dozen sat on a serving plate on the dining table where he had engaged his guests well into the night last evening. But he'd consigned himself to have a taste of only one of Esme's cookies. It was all he could afford. Even though he wanted more. So much more.

He'd never felt so satisfied by a treat before. He felt both full and starved at the same time. He took another bite, just a small one. The cookie crumbled under his teeth. Like an army on the advance, it spread over his tongue and melted without much effort. The bits of sugar positively danced over his taste buds like dancing sparkles.

Dancing sparkles? He put the other half of the cookie down. What was going on with him?

"That will ruin your appetite for the rest of the day."

Leo looked up to see Giles looking down disapprovingly

at the last bite of his cookie. Leo wasn't usually prone to wanting treats or sweets. However, the last piece laying on the plate taunted him, causing his mouth to water with desire. He picked it up and devoured it in one bite.

"It's just a one-time thing," he said. "I won't form a habit."

The last bite was even sweeter and more satisfying. It lingered on his tongue, sticking to the insides of his teeth. He felt every bit of sugar as he swallowed. And then it was gone.

He felt the absence acutely, almost like a missing limb. But he had all his limbs and faculties about him. He looked back to the door where he'd last seen Esme. The need in his stomach migrated to somewhere north in the vicinity of his chest.

He'd never had these feelings before, this intense craving for ... something. Perhaps it was due to his one too many years as a widow. He hadn't engaged in female pleasures since the passing of his wife. He hadn't had the time or inclination. There was always his duty to consider, and his reputation to uphold, and so he'd never indulged.

There had only been Isabel. They'd been engaged since he was six. He'd felt duty bound to her from the moment he understood that girls and boys were different and boys had certain urges. But his promise had been given, albeit by proxy. So, because he'd never felt free to have a taste test, he'd never even considered being with another woman.

He'd cared for his wife, as was his duty. But his heart had never fluttered or warmed at the thought of Isabel. Her taste had never lingered on his tongue, or set a trail as he swallowed her scent, or settled with sugary hooks in his belly.

"I wouldn't begrudge you sowing your royal oats."

It was Giles's words more than the sound of his voice that jerked Leo back to the present.

"But," Giles said, "not in front of the princess or Lady Teresa."

Fire licked over the warmth in Leo's gut. "You overstep your place, Giles. I take grave offense for you thinking I would ever do anything untoward in front of my own child."

"You're a man, majesty," Giles said plainly.

"I thought I was a king."

"And she is a commoner."

Leo opened his mouth. Then closed it. He looked down at his empty plate. There were still a few brown crumbs on the white porcelain. His fingers itched to swipe them off the plate and into his mouth for just another hint of Esme.

"She's also an American." Giles ticked Esme's disqualifications off on his fingers. "She's a school teacher. She lacks any and all knowledge of royal life outside of children's books. She has no qualifications to be a queen."

"She makes Penelope smile." Shouldn't that be a factor in his decision of a wife? His child was his first priority. Shouldn't her new stepmother be chosen with Pea in mind and not the entire country? "And she knows fractions. Mathematics is a necessity in our business."

Giles ground his molars. His face pinched as he appeared to struggle to hold his tongue. It was an anomaly for them both. Leo never stepped an inch off his prescribed path. Giles had never had to scold him, not seriously.

Leo's attraction to Esme was a serious matter. A matter that had no footing in the real world. Leo lifted his napkin to his mouth and dabbed at his lips, removing any excess crumbs from his face.

"Luckily, Lady Teresa excels at numbers and

spreadsheets," he said, placing the napkin over the remaining crumbs on his plate.

Giles breathed a sigh of relief.

There were a few crumbs on his shirt front. He brushed those away too. "Partnering with the Almodovars will be good for business."

"Lady Teresa will be good for you," said Giles. "That is, if you let her in."

Let her in? Leo was prepared to entwine two powerful families. The contracts were being drawn as they spoke. She would have access to his empire. But he knew that wasn't the access Giles spoke of.

"Cookies for breakfast?" Alex came into the dining area, looking surprisingly put together. He'd gone out before the dinner party was over and hadn't slinked back into the suite until the early morning hours. "Is it my birthday or are people finally reading my memos?"

Alex swiped two cookies off the plate and plunked one and then the other into his mouth. "These are delicious."

"Pea made them," said Leo. He swatted at his brother's hand before he could steal more. "Save some for your niece."

"I'll miss this American cuisine with their overuse of sugar and fats," said Alex around a mouthful of a third cookie. "If I could snag an American baker for the Union Day pie competition, I'd be a shoe in against the Duke of Mondego and whatever French chef he brings in this year."

"The two of you still have that rivalry? Over pies? Seriously, when will you grow up?"

"There is no law that says I have to." Alex licked his fingers making a vein pop out of Giles's neck. Leo was certain that's why his brother did it. They both had impeccable table manners. "I wonder if I could get the recipe for that pie from last night? A creation like that would demolish any competition."

Leo perked up at the thought of pie. Specifically, at the thought of a particular pie shop which just so happened to be walking distance from a certain kindergarten teacher's school. His stomach grumbled with want.

"You know," Leo tried for a casual tone, "it's on the way to the airport. I could swing by and grab one before we're due to board."

From the corner of his gaze, he saw Giles bristle. Leo licked his bottom lip. All trace of any sweetness was gone. It was just as well.

"On second thought," Leo said. "I don't have the time in my schedule."

Leo took his covered plate from the table and left the room. He made his way into the kitchen where the staff had cleaned all trace of the flour fairies' shenanigans from the room. He placed the dish under the faucet and washed the crumbs down the drain.

Sweets were fine. Every once in a while. But he had always enjoyed a healthy diet. It was time to get on from dessert and plan his main course.

CHAPTER TWELVE

The one good thing about the Global Learning Preparatory Academy, aside from their generous catering budgets on teacher workdays, was the copious amounts of school breaks. GLPA took every holiday off, and that included all religious and cultural observances. The powers that be at the school were overly cautious as to not offend any of their enrolled families who happily forked over the high-priced admission fees and tuition.

This long weekend of a Thursday and Fridday off were courtesy of United Nations Day. Though not a National American holiday, it was instituted by the UN which asked its member countries to celebrate. The United States did the courtesy of putting the day on the calendar but didn't upgrade it to the federal level.

Banks would be open. Parking meters would still tick. Most public schools would be open, but not GLPA. The students and staff would take those two days to celebrate the diversity of its school population by staying home. Surprisingly, the working parents at GLPA weren't pleased.

"Miss Picket."

Esme took a deep, calming breath at the grating sound of Principal Clarke's voice. She glanced over her shoulder, only offering her profile and not her full attention. The move cranked the nape of her neck.

"Are you sure you can't work during the break?" he asked walking toward her.

This year, one of the parents, Aubrey Thomas's mother, had suggested that during some of the breaks, like this one, the school offer supplementary learning programs for their students. The new program came with a nice bonus check for those teachers who offered their services. Esme had considered it, but that was before ... the thing.

"Most of our staff have husbands and children," Principal Clarke continued. "They'll be celebrating their own unions. And you ..." He cleared his throat and looked down.

The pain in her neck increased in the unnatural twist, but she didn't turn to face him. She was headed out the door and not looking back. She needed these extra days to recuperate.

Esme had gotten herself a stack of books, loaded up her Amazon Prime video shelf with Jane Austen movie adaptations, and was prepared for a girls' weekend with Jan.

Along with pie. There would be lots of pie. It was just what she needed to get over the thing that would never be with a king that was beyond her realm.

Starting this weekend when, whenever she saw Colin Firth's face or Hugh Grant's face, she would picture Leo's dark, good looks. When the movies faded to black after a proper happily ever after, she'd likely cry. But at least she could press rewind and experience the feelings all over again on repeat.

That would not be happening in real life as the king of

her dreams was likely on a plane to a faraway land. He hadn't run after her as she entered the elevator. He hadn't been standing outside her door this morning. He hadn't come to the pie shop at lunch. It was over.

"I'm afraid I'm unavailable, Principal Clarke. I'll see you next week." And with that, Esme untwisted herself and reached for the door. Unfortunately, the pain in her neck didn't cease.

"Before I forget," he called after her, "this was just sent over this morning."

The envelope he handed her had the mark of Cordoba; a regal lion with its claws extended that had the lower body of a fish. Esme's heart skipped a beat. Maybe it wasn't a dream after all. Maybe it was her invitation to the ball this weekend at Cordoba's Union Day. It was a fat envelope. A goodbye, just like a college rejection letter, would be thin.

She stepped outside and carefully peeled at the corners of the delicate envelope. She wanted to keep it as a memento of how their love story began. But little tears heeded her progress. Until finally, she tore the expensive paper apart.

A short note tumbled out. When she opened it, she saw the neat script.

Thank you for the math and cooking lesson, HRH Penelope Antoinette Marguerite Almeria.

A cookie tumbled out of the envelope as well. Nothing else.

Esme flipped the note over. Nothing.

She turned the torn envelope inside out. Nothing.

She peered again at the neat, grammatically perfect script. Could a five-year-old write this? Penelope was exceptional for her age. Maybe her father had helped her? Maybe he had written it? But wouldn't he have signed it too?

But he hadn't. She was back at square one. Literally. She'd walked the two blocks from the school to the pie shop and now stood on the street where she and Leo had first met.

She waited for the walk sign, looking up and down at the cars stopped at the light. There were no dragon cleaning trucks in sight. No royal town cars, either. It was safe to cross.

Esme pushed through the pie shop doors. She needed a savory treat and fast. But she came up short once inside.

A familiar dark head leaned his body against the counter. His dark hair lay in haphazard waves on his regal head. His hazel eyes sparkled with delight, but also a hint of mischief. He turned and gave Esme a brilliant smile that would've dazzled the common woman. Esme was unfazed.

"Your majesty." Esme stopped before the royal figure and executed an awkward bow.

"No," said Prince Alexander. "I'm not majestic. Just highness. But please, don't call me that out in public here in America. It's just Alex amongst friends."

Friends? When had that happened? He'd barely spoken a few sentences to her.

"What are you doing here, Alex?" Esme looked around. But there was no dark haired king tucked away in any of the pie shop's booths.

"I'm trying to convince our other friend here to enter a pie making contest."

"Pie making contest?" Esme looked to Jan and couldn't help but smile.

The two women stood before a real live prince, a charming one at that. But neither of them were swooning. Not Esme, because she had other interests. Not Jan, because she had no interest.

With Jan's history, Esme seriously doubted the pie maker would ever find herself in another relationship that didn't involve blended butter and dough. If Prince Alex was looking to get Jan's help by using something other than his magnetic personality, it wouldn't hold, because Jan was not attracted.

"As you know, bisteeva is the national dish of Cordoba," he laid out the facts. "There's an annual pie making contest happening this weekend. It comes with major bragging rights for the winner."

"You want me to give you my recipe?" asked Jan.

"No, no," Alex laughed. "I can't cook in the competition."

"Why not?" asked Jan. Her right eyebrow tilted up in suspicion as though she smelled something foul. Since being left at the altar a couple years ago, Jan had developed a truly infallible bologna meter.

"I ..." The Prince of Cordoba faltered, looking unsure of himself probably for the first time in his life.

"From the five-minute conversation we just had," said Jan, "you seem to certainly know your way around food."

"I do." He smiled, almost sheepishly. And in the same instant, the sheep went home, and the roguish wolf came back out to play. "But I can't enter the contest. I'm a prince. So each year, I scour the globe to find the best pastry chef to enter this competition. I had Joseph Hayden lined up but—"

"Joseph Hayden?" Jan's skeptical facade slipped, and her eyes went as wide as a pie tin. "James Beard award-winning chef Joseph Hayden?"

Like a fisherman who knew he had hooked something on his line, Alex leaned closer and tugged. "After tasting your pie the other day, I called and told him I'd found my ringer."

"Me?" Jan pressed her hand to her chest. "I'm your ringer?"

"But of course, if you don't feel up to it ..." Alex leaned back and shoved his hands in his pockets. His eyes fell to Esme. "And of course, your friend can come too."

Oh, he was good. He was very good. So good that Esme danced on his string and pulled Jan aside.

"You know we're going," she said.

"I can't leave the country," said Jan. "I have a business to run. Besides, neither of us can afford it."

"Did I mention it's at no expense to either of you," said Alex. "I'll fly you out for the weekend. You can stay in the castle as my guest."

In the castle? With the king?

"Oh," Alex continued. "I should also make you aware that there is a monetary prize for winning the competition. It's small. I believe just five grand or so."

Jan truly resembled a fish out of water. Her mouth opened and closed but nothing came out. Esme knew her friend needed the money. Despite how much customers loved her pies, she just didn't have enough business these days.

"You'd retain it all," said Alex. "I just want the bragging rights. The Duke of Mondego and I have a bit of a rivalry, you see."

"Duke?" said Esme. "There are kings, princes, and dukes in Cordoba?"

"Dukes, marquises, earls, viscounts, barons, lords and ladies we have them all. And, I know a certain princess would be delighted if a certain kindergarten teacher came."

Alex turned his attention to Esme as if she needed more convincing. She was already planning her wardrobe.

"You've made quite the impression on Pea," he said.

"Those cookies were the best math I've ever tasted. What do you two say?"

Esme looked to Jan. She pleaded with her eyes. When Jan still hesitated, Esme pressed her hands together in prayer.

Finally, Jan sighed. "Two tickets to paradise."

"Pack your bags, we leave tonight," said Alex. "You've got about six hours before wheels up on the royal jet. Plenty of time to get your affairs in order."

The two women looked at each other in horror, true doubt finally crossing both of their faces. Plenty of time for a man to pack, maybe. But two single women going overseas to a land filled with royalty? This was a crisis fit for a fairy godmother. Unfortunately, neither Esme nor Jan had one.

CHAPTER THIRTEEN

"Here, let me help you with that."

Leo reached for Lady Teresa's designer luggage. He considered himself a strong man. He had never been the type of monarch to simply sit on a throne. He was an active man and visited the gym every day. Sure, the gym was an actual gymnasium in the west wing of his castle. So, there should be no trouble with him lifting a woman's suitcase.

He gripped the handle of the suitcase and gave a tug. It did not budge. He gave it a shove in an attempt to tilt it onto its rolling wheels. It stayed upright. Before he could wonder if the future Duchess of Almodovar had made off with an American bronzed statue, she stayed his hand.

"No need," she said. "My father's valet's got it."

The valet in question, a strapping man with muscles bulging out of his dark jacket, used two fingers to tip the case over on its side. Then he picked it up, one handed, and carried both it and Lady Teresa's slightly smaller carry-on away.

Leo rubbed at his arms. He may have given the muscles

there a squeeze just to make sure they were still there. Luckily, Teresa had missed that display, or lack thereof, of royal masculinity. Her nose was in her handheld, tapping away.

"Are you sure I can't give you a ride across the pond?" Leo chucked his thumb toward his private jet. Spain was just a hop, skip, and a jump from Cordoba.

"No need," said Teresa, without looking up. "I've got my own family jet." She chucked her own thumb at the jet next to his. Then she tapped a few more keys on her phone. "And I've got to stop over in London for an afternoon meeting with Sir Jorge Barry."

"Ah, Jorgey. I know him. We went to school together."

"I know him too. We dated a few years back or so." With a few more taps on her phone, she finally slid the device in her purse and looked up. Her head tilted to the side like an inquisitive bird. "Don't tell me you're the jealous type?"

"No, I'm not."

He wasn't. Not jealous, anyway. He struggled to understand what he was feeling.

Perhaps annoyance. But why?

Leo glanced up at the valet handing the luggage into the aircraft. One handed. He looked down at the highly successful, highly connected woman he was considering making his wife.

Did she even need him at all? What exactly was he bringing into this merger? Other than his title, lands, and waterways?

"I'm very excited about our venture," she said. "I look forward to getting to know you better, your majesty."

"You can call me Leo."

"I will now that I have your permission. Leo."

Lady Teresa grinned. It was a lovely grin. She was a lovely woman.

They were still strangers. It would take time for them to become comfortable with one another. Leo had had years with his first wife. He needed to give this new courtship a few weeks, maybe even months.

"So, I'll see you in a couple of days for the gala," she said, pulling her phone from her purse and tapping buttons once more.

"I'll be the one in the crown," he said.

Lady Teresa looked up. She tilted her head to the side again and blinked.

"It was a joke," he said.

"I know," she smiled. "I just assumed you were a serious man."

"I let my hair down every once in a while."

She laughed at that causing Leo to grin. Thank goodness she had a sense of humor. Not that Leo cracked a lot of jokes. But he did want a different relationship this time, a warm one.

Maybe it wouldn't take as long as he thought for them to become comfortable with one another. Maybe they could even start right now. When they'd said goodnight last night it had been with a curtsey on her part and a kiss to the knuckles on his. Maybe this time, it could be more.

Leo leaned in.

Lady Teresa blinked. Her head straightened. Then tilted.

Leo tilted his head to the opposite side so that when he landed, his lips would perfectly align with hers. But at the same moment, Lady Teresa straightened her head.

It was a slow descent. And just like a plane coming in for a rocky landing and needing air traffic control to guide their wings, Leo and Teresa spent a little bit of time with their heads tilting slightly left, then right, until …

How could their teeth meet before their lips? Then their noses mashed. All before their lips even met. It had to have been the worst kiss in history.

It was too late to adjust. Leo pulled back as she leaned forward. Now they both were leaning back. At least the crash landing had left no casualties.

"That was awkward," Lady Teresa said.

"Yeah," he grimaced.

"But better than my first kiss with Jorgey."

It lightened the mood, but Leo was still horrified. "I shouldn't have assumed I even could kiss you," he said. "A ride to the airport isn't exactly a first date."

"In our world, a limo ride to my jet is the high point of courtship."

"Now we're going promenading around the park, but we'll be in international airspace."

Lady Teresa smiled at that. She did have a lovely smile. She leaned in again. This time, Leo held his ground, uncertain exactly where this was going.

Teresa pressed her lips just to the side of his mouth. Leo breathed her in. There was that pleasant scent again, of warm cinnamon. He could easily get used to it. He could be content to spend the rest of his days breathing it in. He could look forward to feeling her slightly firm lips pressed just off to the side of his. They would have a good life, a comfortable partnership.

"Safe travels, Leonidas."

"You too, Teresa."

He watched her walk away and into her jet. The belly of the gray beast swallowed her up and began its taxi. His possible betrothed was traveling on her own steel horse. Leo turned to his.

But not before giving America one last look. The sky was a riot of purples and pinks as day turned to night. The sun was fast setting on this adventure. It was time to get back to his real world, tucked away on an island paradise filled with royal responsibilities.

He nodded to the pilot as he boarded the plane. His support staff always sat at the front of the plane while he and his family occupied the back. He hadn't traveled with much staff on this venture, just Giles, a few security personnel, and an aide to help with Penelope. Most of them were already on board and inclined their heads as he passed.

As he made his way back to his section, the aisle was blocked with a huge piece of luggage that would never fit into the overhead compartment. A woman with a shapely figure struggled with another case that was of similar size, trying to shove it in.

As Leo reached up to help her, her case fell. Instead of reaching for the case, he reached for her, pulling her out of harm's way and into his arms. The moment his skin touched hers, warmth spread through him at the contact, like the sun dawning on a new day.

"Esme?"

"Hey, Leo."

CHAPTER FOURTEEN

*E*sme saw stars. Tiny little bits of fireworks rained down before her eyes like those handheld sparkles on the Fourth of July. Little, blue songbirds chirped a lulling love song in her ears. Her entire body tingled with electricity. All from being back inside Leo's embrace.

He gazed down at her. In his hazel eyes, she saw sparkles reflecting back at her. He let out a tiny sigh that sounded every bit like a bird's song. The touch of his finger pads on her bare skin made her wonder if they were flying too close to the sun.

Esme hadn't imagined it. There it was, standing between them. The thing.

Leo's gaze dipped to her lips in the universal language of I desperately want to kiss you.

But he didn't kiss her. He blinked. Then he righted her, placing her feet firmly back on the ground. He took a step back until he was on the opposite side of the aisle from her.

Behind him in the window, Esme saw that night had fallen. Lights of other planes taking off and descending lit up the sky. Chirps and beeps came from the pilots preparing in the cockpit. The air had come on in the private plane producing the goosebumps on her arm.

"What are you doing here?" Leo asked.

"Alex invited me."

Something in his face changed. His gaze narrowed. His fingers gripped the tops of the chairs. "You're here with Alex?"

"Alex invited Jan. The pie maker. For the baking contest."

Relief flooded his face. "You're just here dropping off your friend."

Esme's breath stuck in her chest, never quite reaching her belly. It was just as well because her belly was tensing in knots. Uncertainty begged her to keep her mouth shut. But her heart ignored the thought.

"Well," she said, "I'm coming, too."

"Coming to Cordoba?"

She nodded.

"For the weekend."

She nodded again.

Leo gulped. His Adam's apple rose and fell along his throat column. He looked back to the front of the plane as though searching for an escape.

"I hope I'm not intruding or overstepping any bounds, your majesty."

His attention snapped back to her at the mention of the honorific. Hope blossomed. But he didn't insist that she call him Leo like before.

Instead, they stood staring at one another. Esme with hope in her gaze. Leo with something that looked very much like wariness in his.

"Evening, brother. Hey there, teach." Alex ambled his way down the aisle, followed by Jan. Neither got far with

Esme's suitcase still blocking the path. "You need help with that?"

Before Alex could reach for her case, Leo came out of his sequestered spot in the opposing seats. He hefted her bag up and over his head. Esme had worried the piece of luggage wouldn't fit, but Leo maneuvered it until it slid into place. His muscles bulged and flexed as he did so. Esme did not look away.

"You all set there?" Alex asked her.

"Yes," she said. "Thank you, your highness."

"We talked about this. It's Alex. You're practically family." He gave her a squeeze on the shoulder.

Behind Alex, Leo's breath caught. Perhaps it was the physical exertion of lifting her suitcase, but there it was again. The thing.

Leo swallowed. The bob of the projection on his neck was even more pronounced. It looked like he couldn't dispose of whatever it was he was trying to get rid of.

"Don't be flattered by my brother's overtures," said Leo. "Anyone who feeds him he considers family."

"If that were true, then I'm likely to marry our Chef Jan here."

Jan cringed at the thought. For a second, Alex actually looked taken aback, as though he couldn't fathom any woman not dying to be his princess. If ever there was such a woman, it would be Jan. She had no plans to ever don a veil again after her first and only disaster with matrimony.

Leo chuckled at Jan's grimace. When he did, his breath touched Esme's nose. Now it was Esme's turn to swallow. Unlike Leo, she gulped the taste of him down.

Leo watched the movement of Esme's lips. Esme could've sworn she saw him grit his teeth. It didn't look like annoyance. It looked like desperation.

He didn't want to be attracted to her. It was classic Jane Austen. She was Elizabeth, and he was Mr. Darcy. Finally, she knew how the story was supposed to go. Esme breathed a sigh of relief which was stunted by the clearing of a throat.

"Your majesty, your highness." Giles looked at them from the back of the plane. "We'll be taking off soon. Best to take your seats."

Giles made a sweeping motion to the back of the plane where the royal party sat. There had been a curtain there, but it was swept aside. It was first class in reverse.

"Ms. Picket?" Penelope appeared through the curtain. "I'm so happy you're here."

The child smiled wide, but she kept her hands together in front of her. Esme couldn't shake that the girl looked like a miniature version of an adult in her cardigan and pale dress. This late in the day, she was still perfectly put together, not a hair out of place.

"I am too." Esme smiled. "I'd love to present to you my best friend, Jan Peppers. She's a baker."

"She must be excellent at fractions," quipped Princess Penelope.

"Indeed, she is."

"Perhaps we can bake together?" said Penelope.

"I'd like that," Jan replied.

"I wouldn't want her to get in the way," said Leo.

"She wouldn't be in the way at all," said Jan. "Little helpers have the best hands. Maybe you can help us? As a child, you must get to eat lots of pastries. I'd love to hear about your favorite Cordovian pastries to help me prepare for the pie making competition."

"We're about to take off," Giles said. "The princess needs to take her seat."

"Can't I sit here with Ms. Pickett and her friend?" Princess Penelope looked to her father for permission.

"Your highness, your place is in here with the royal family," said Giles. But he looked to Leo as he spoke.

Ouch. If she hadn't sussed it out already, Esme pegged Giles as the villain of this particular tale. He might be armed with a scowl and a superior attitude, but Esme had hundreds of years of literature and dozens of animated musicals on her side.

Still, it stung, and she cast her gaze downward. That was the only reason she saw Leo's fingers ball into fists. He didn't swallow anything down this time. His voice was resonating and commanding.

"If the princess would like to spend her time learning math and entertaining our guests, then so be it."

Leo chucked his daughter under the chin. Then he lifted his gaze to Esme. He opened his mouth. Then closed it and tried again. "Just let me know if she becomes a bother."

"With such perfect manners, I doubt that's even possible."

With another glance at Esme's lips, Leo turned his back and was gone. For now.

Esme strapped into her seat with a smile. As the plane taxied onto the runway, she prepared herself for the part of the story where her life changed forever.

CHAPTER FIFTEEN

The unfasten your seatbelt sign came on overhead followed by a message from the pilot about the expected duration of their flight. Leo did not unfasten his belt. He needed the extra security to ensure that he stayed put. With the curtains still pulled back, Leo was able to see into the staff section of the plane.

Alex sat with Jan, the pie maker. The two put their heads together, likely talking spices and sweetmeats. Jan quirked an eyebrow at the prince every now and again. But more often than not, a look of consideration crossed her features, followed by a small smile, and a reluctant nod of agreement. For resisting his brother's charms, Leo decided he liked the woman even more.

Two of the flight attendants hovered about just outside of their view. Those two gazed down at Alex in the way women often did his brother as though he were a priceless handbag or pair of shoes that they knew they couldn't afford but still hoped for. Alex was entirely focused on Jan and the piece of paper they passed back and forth between them. Food was his brother's only passion. Unfortunately, there was little way to exercise a passion for the culinary arts for a prince.

Then there was his little Penelope. She gazed up, her eyes shining bright, her smile wide and genuine. Leo couldn't remember the last time he saw his daughter smiling in pure joy. His gaze traveled over to see why. He knew the source before his gaze landed on her.

Esme grinned down at his daughter as though Penelope were a flower blooming. Plenty of women were nice to Penelope. Be it because of her status or because of her relation to him. But Esme had taken his daughter under her wing before she knew he had any attachment to Penelope.

In the kitchen, and even now, Esme gave Penelope her full, unadulterated attention. Esme had a small smile on her face with just one corner of her lips lifted. It was her amused smile.

Wow, had he already begun to learn the woman's smiles?

Yes, he had. He knew that when she leaned in with her hand on her chin; she was considering what had just been said to her. He knew that if she tugged at her lower lip with her thumb and index finger; she was waiting to talk. He knew that her eyes squinted when telling a tale and then everyone else would lean in.

Yes, he knew her looks, her expressions, her motions.

"The duke's not winning this year," said Alex as he slunk down into the seat next to Leo. "Jan is going to crush whatever second rate chef he brings in. The woman's a genius."

It took Leo a moment to focus on his brother and his words. Alex and the Duke of Mondego had a long standing rivalry. It stemmed from them being two of the youngest royals with wealth and good looks. They constantly needed to find new ways to one up each other, be it a swimming competition, racing sports cars, on down to who found the best chef to win a pie making competition.

It was juvenile. But Alex could be in to worse things. So, Leo didn't complain. Still, he'd pulled the pie maker across the ocean to participate in his little sparring contest.

"Is it really so important that you win that you have to drag people from their lives like play things?" said Leo.

"I invited two women to an island paradise for the weekend. When would they ever have an opportunity like this?"

"So, you're calling them beneath you?"

Alex opened his mouth. Then appeared to think better of speaking his first thought. "Which is it? Am I inconsiderate or ignorant?"

Leo sighed and turned away from his brother. Alex could be a pest of a little brother when he wanted to. He leaned over to Leo and kept buzzing in his ear.

"I thought you liked Esme." When Leo didn't respond Alex buzzed closer. "Oh, I see. You *like* Esme. Perhaps a little too much."

Leo reached for his seatbelt but still didn't trust himself with freedom. He yanked headphones from the side of the seat and plunked them over his head. Unfortunately, he forgot to plug them in. The cable dangled over his knee for Alex to see and know that Leo could still hear every word he said.

"This is great," said Alex. "It's finally happened. You have a crush on a girl."

"Stop it," Leo commanded, peering into the front of the plane to see if they'd been overheard. No one looked up. And Alex kept going because Leo's powers of state didn't extend to his brother.

"Well, we'll have to have The Talk."

"There will be no talk," Leo growled. "There will be no anything. I'm practically engaged."

"But you're not." Alex's face sobered. He placed a hand on Leo's shoulder and, for one of the few times in his life, looked earnest. "It doesn't have to be the same as it was before. It doesn't have to be a business arrangement. It could be something more."

"Has my little playboy of a brother suddenly become a romantic?" Leo snorted, trying but failing to brush his brother's hand from his shoulder.

"I wouldn't go that far," said Alex. "But I do want what's best for you. You deserve happiness. Especially with all you do for everyone else."

Leo brushed the notion off. "Marriage has been done this way amongst royals for centuries."

"Until good old cousin Henry and his harem of revolving wives."

"That's your example? Henry the Eighth was not an honorable man."

"There's always Edward the Eighth who abdicated for love."

"There is another option," Leo hedged.

"Don't even think about it." Alex held up his hand before Leo could even get any more words out. "Me on the throne?"

Alex shuddered.

So did Leo.

Leo always hoped he'd have the luck of Prince Phillip of England. Phillip was chosen as a suitor for Princess Elizabeth when she was just five years old. Luckily for them, they fell in love and reigned happily ever after to this day.

Leo and Isabel hadn't been in love. They'd never pretended that could be between them. But maybe, just maybe, it was possible with Lady Teresa? He just had to give it a try.

Now he at least had an inkling of what that sensation might feel like. His gaze went to Esme again. Just the sight of her and butterflies flapped around in his heart.

He shook himself, turning back to his brother. "We've always had different responsibilities, you and I."

"Not really," said Alex. "Our only requirement is to live life to the fullest and pay taxes. But we beat the latter game and get paid by taxes. No reason you can't live a full life now that you're solely in charge of it."

"Be serious."

"I am," said Alex. "No one's arranging your life but you."

"We need an alliance for Cordoba's future."

"Sometimes I wonder if instead of rescuing a damsel in distress, you need to be rescued from yourself."

With a final pat on the shoulder, Alex turned over and, in an instant, he was asleep. In a matter of moments, so was everyone else. Except Leo.

The King of Cordoba stayed awake and watched Penelope who fell asleep against Esme's shoulder. He watched Esme shift in her sleep and bring his daughter into the cradle of her embrace.

The move tugged hard at Leo's heart strings, shaking off the butterflies and turning them into something else. Something bigger. Perhaps birds?

He didn't know. He just knew the rumbling they made inside of his chest wouldn't let him close his eyes. And so he watched over the two of them as they flew through the sky.

CHAPTER SIXTEEN

"M s. Pickett, wake up. We're nearly there."

Esme's eyes fluttered open. Slowly, a round cherubic face came into view. The little angel had the most beautiful hazel eyes. There were sparkles in the pupils. The little girl looked as pretty as a princess. Even after six hours of flying, Penelope still looked entirely put together, not a hair out of place, not a wrinkle in her clothes. It couldn't be anything but magic.

"Look." Penelope pointed out the window. "This is my favorite part."

Esme sat up. Her contorted bones crackled and snapped. Then her eyes popped out of her head as she turned and looked out the window. It was a storybook illustration come to life. Like the bird from *The Lion King* flying out of the mist and down onto Pride Rock. Only on the rock sat a castle that put the Disney Cinderella Castle to shame.

The clouds parted to reveal a lush green land. Set against the backdrop of the rising sun, which turned the sky various shades of pink and lavender, rose a white castle.

Brick battlements bordered one side from the sea. Silver and gold capped towers and turrets reached for the sky.

"It looks like magic," Esme breathed.

"Our ancestors were an eclectic and flashy bunch," said the five-year-old, surprising Esme once again with her grasp of the English language. "They were Moors from Africa, Spanish conquistadors, and French aristocrats, with a few English cousins coming along during the Middle Ages."

"People would pay just for the view," said Jan, leaning over to catch a glimpse for herself.

"It's hard to get here for the average person." Alex rejoined their bunch, taking his former seat beside Jan.

"You could start a cruise line from Spain or France," said Esme.

Esme looked up to see Leo cock his head at her words. He stood at the curtained barrier between the common class and the royal line. Unlike his brother, Leo did not come across into their territory.

After a tight smile and nod at Esme, he turned his attention to his daughter. "Buckle up, Sweet Pea. We're about to land."

And with that, he turned and took his seat in the back. His head went down to look over papers. He only looked up to talk to Giles. He did not look in Esme's direction again.

As they moved closer to the landing field, the castle disappeared from view. Esme's heart ached to see the structure up close, to experience the magic she'd seen from afar in real life. She settled back into her seat and waited to have her feet on the ground once more.

The landing was as smooth as the flight. Once the unbuckle your seatbelt sign came on, Esme bolted out of her seat, eager to see this extraordinary world with her own eyes. But first, she had to win the battle of her oversized suitcases.

She managed to free her first piece. But the second case was determined to stay on the plane. Though she hadn't heard the sound of his steps, she felt his presence before he made himself known. Before he asked, Esme stepped aside to allow Leo to hand down her luggage.

He handled the task with ease. When he was done, and the wheels of her luggage were on the floor, he didn't look up at her. He turned as though to leave.

"Your homeland looks beautiful from the sky," she said to his back. "I can't wait to see it on foot."

He gave her a polite nod. His gaze was fixed on her shoulder and not her face.

Esme had seen this scene play out in countless romantic comedies. The hero was doing everything he could to put distance between himself and the woman who was clearly right for him. Esme just needed him to look into her eyes again. Then he'd see the truth of the matter. He'd see the thing.

"I don't suppose you have time to show us around?"

"No." He fixed the cuff links on his shirt. "I'm afraid I don't have time today."

"Oh. Of course. Perhaps I'll see you later at dinner?"

He shook his head, now adjusting his watch. "There's much to do before the gala."

"I'm sorry." Now she looked down. She was losing this battle, and she was out of ideas. "I'm on vacation, but you're back to work."

He'd stopped fiddling with his watch. His fingers were still, but he wasn't moving forward. Esme chanced a glance up and their gazes connected. Only for a second, but that was all it took. The spark reignited, burning brighter than before.

Leo gulped, but just like before he couldn't swallow that look of desire past his Adam's apple. He cursed under his breath and took a step toward her. "This may look like a fairytale to you, but it's my real life."

There was a note of desperation in his voice when he spoke to her. A pleading in his gaze for her to understand. She did understand.

She understood that the feelings she was certain he was developing for her were inconvenient. She understood that he was increasingly powerless to do anything about them as they grew. She understood all of this because she felt the same way.

She didn't say any of that. She didn't need to. She knew that it was as clear to him as it was to her. She simply had no plans to resist it.

"If I don't see much of you over the next few days ... I hope you enjoy your time here in my homeland."

He inclined his head. He turned on his heel. And then he was gone.

"Ah, you don't want him to show you around," said Alex. "He'll take you to the state house to see where our laws are made, or to the mint where our money is printed, possibly even some battlefields. All boring things."

"Not for a teacher," said Esme.

Alex grimaced, as though he'd forgotten Esme's profession. "Well, then you definitely need an expert on the fun things to do in Cordoba. Please allow me to be your guide."

"May I come too, Uncle Alex?" asked Penelope.

"Of course," he said. "It's high time you study the fine art of royal recreation."

"Are you sure," said Esme. "We don't want to take you off your schedule or be a bother."

"My job as the second-born son is to traipse around the country and look good while doing it. You could look it up. It's a constitutional law."

"It is not," giggled Penelope.

"Well, they'll never know that because we're not going to the state house."

CHAPTER SEVENTEEN

"Wonderful job with your speech the other day, your majesty. I'm given to understand the Almodovars approached you about joining with their maritime enterprise?"

"That's not all I hear they want to join with, our good king."

A round of guffaws sounded around Leo's office in the east wing of the palace. Looking up from his desk he saw a line of rotund torsos shaking in a cringe worthy mockery of out of shape belly dancers. Much of the nobility were older men who'd grown fat on the wealth their status and their ancient fortunes provided them. But also in the room sat many of these men's sons, the next generation who would take over as gout and heart disease claimed their father's in the end.

"Did you not speak at all of agricultural trade during your time in the states, King Leo?" the soon to be Baron of Balansya asked.

The blond-haired, baby-faced man was by far the

youngest in the room; a year or two younger than Alex, if Leo remembered correctly. The current Baron of Balansya was at present bedridden, but still grasping firm to his title. Balansya was one of the most fertile regions in all of Cordoba, with coffee beans being their best crop.

"I didn't only speak with the Almodovars about maritime opportunities," said Leo. "I reached out to a number of other countries and industry leaders. Many will be at this weekend's Union Day celebration."

"Excellent," smiled the young baron in training.

In Leo's mind, the training wheels were ready to come off, and the man could, and should, take full ownership of his family's lands before his father ran what little profit remained into the ground.

"What about the Almodovar woman?" pushed another of the old guard.

"Yes, are we expecting a new queen soon?"

These grown men were like teen girls gossiping at the lunch table. Leo could tell them that he and Lady Teresa had met and had a connection, of sorts. He could tell them that she'd agreed to come visit and pursue their potential relationship this weekend. But his mouth stayed shut for some unfathomable reason.

"I still say my daughter is the best option," said the Duke of Ebra.

"Your daughter is sixteen years old," said the Viscount of Jucar.

The baron's son discreetly pulled out his cell phone and began texting. Leo doubted it was to any friend or paramour. The young man was likely looking up stock prices of coffee beans. Coffee he could have with any girl he wanted, being a baron and not a king.

Leo noted the Earl of Larida sitting in a corner with his head in a book as per usual. Daniel would read the ketchup bottle if it were the only thing available in the room with printed words. He and Esme would get along perfectly. Both liked to live in made up worlds rather than the reality. Earls didn't have quite the same restrictions as kings either. Daniel was free to marry whomever he chose, within a certain degree. But that degree was more than Leo had.

"Is the fate of our great nation boring you, Larida?" asked Leo.

"Oh, no. Not at all. Carry on." Daniel didn't even bother to look up. He waved his hand, and his head disappeared entirely in the book.

"I just figured you might have something to add to this conversation?"

"About your intended bride, agricultural trade, maritime expansion, or statutory rape?"

Leo bit his tongue so that he didn't chuckle. He should've known his friend had caught every word of the conversations around him. Daniel simply wasn't interested in them.

The man was lucky they were close friends or Leo would throw him in the dungeons. But that would likely be a vacation for him. Sitting in a cell where no one would bother him. He could read all day and night to his heart's content.

"If that's all, gentlemen," Leo said. The phrase was a statement, not a question, that meant he was done with this audience. It was Leo's favorite power as king. Besides, he did have a full schedule for the rest of the day that didn't include entertaining the nosey lords of the realm.

As the room cleared out, Leo leaned back in his desk

chair. It was his great grandfather's desk, but his father's chair. Inheriting the desk made him aware of his responsibilities to this country, to his people, to his family. But the chair was what let him know that he was king.

He'd come in here often as a child, sit quietly in a corner and watch his father conduct business of the state. He was always quiet and watchful.

Outside the window, he heard giggling and laughter. Leo stood and peeked out the curtains. He saw the lush gardens his great grandmother had had installed. Guarding it along the path were stone dragons, a gift from Asian royalty that had once visited the island over a hundred years ago. Though the dragons were all in need of repair. He added that to his list.

Finally, he found the source of the laughter. It wasn't Esme. It was other children. He recognized a few as children of nobles who were staying in the castle for Union Day, including the Duke of Ebra's teenage daughter. The girl smiled at a child, and Leo caught sight of her braces.

He shuddered and pulled back from the curtains, but not before seeing a few younger boys at play. He remembered a time when he, Daniel, and Omar, the Marquis of Navarre, would run, and laugh, and play.

They never played knights. They played soldiers as was part of their training as nobles. They never rescued damsels. Well, Daniel had brought it up once before being laughed down by Leo and Omar.

Though the two could marry whomever they chose, Daniel and Omar were still expected to make a good match. Twenty years later, neither the marquis nor the earl had tied the knot even once.

Back down in the gardens, the boys chased each other, nearly knocking down the two older girls. The girls giggled.

But when an adult came into view, they all straightened up, just like good, noble children were trained from birth to do.

Whenever his mother or father came near, Leo would also wipe the smile off his face and put on the blank expression expected of him. Penelope had learned to do the same. But not these past two days.

His daughter grinned ear to ear when she was with Esme. So did Leo. Except today, when he had to turn his back on her.

He had no choice. The more time he spent with Esme, the more he forgot his blank stare. The more time he was near her, he craved the next time they'd be together.

It was easy for him to imagine Pea and Esme laughing and giggling. They were likely somewhere in the city holding hands and having a fine time without him. Esme's eyes were likely wide with wonder. Of course, they were. She was living inside a fairytale.

She hadn't noticed the poverty encroaching around the corner, or the repairs needed on the roads, or the politics brimming under the surface of it all. It was all magic to her.

"You're not yourself."

Leo turned to find that Daniel had remained behind. He'd closed his book and was studying his oldest friend.

Leo shrugged and turned back to the window. "I can never be anyone else."

"Am I going mad, or is Leonidas Almeria waxing philosophic? That's my role, and you can't have it."

Now that they were alone, Leo did drop his royal facade and grinned. Daniel looked at him expectantly. But Leo wasn't ready to tell the tale of the king and the kindergarten teacher. As long as he hadn't started the tale, he never had to admit to the inevitable ending.

"It was just a long trip," he said. "And now duty calls."

"It always does," said Daniel. "As the king, you can decide when and what to answer."

Having been king for more than five years now, Leo knew that wasn't true. He answered every call his country put forth to him. It was his responsibility, and he would not fail.

CHAPTER EIGHTEEN

ordoba was as close to a fairytale in real life as Esme would ever get. They'd spent the morning driving along the coast to see the fortress built to protect the early inhabitants from Spanish attacks from the west and French attacks from the north. The fortresses looked like mini castles. They were no longer inhabited by guards but were renovated into tourist attractions for the beachgoers.

They made it to the city by the early afternoon. Esme's jaw dropped with delight when she saw that some people still rode on horseback. Others in golf carts and small European cars. In and out wove bicycles and pedestrians down the cobbled lanes where tables and tents lined the walkway like a bazaar.

Beyond the bazaar, at the end of the street, were a high street of expensive shops. There were also common staples like The Gap and Old Navy.

After lunch, when they were making their way to the castle, Esme couldn't help but notice the abundance of gardens and parks everywhere. It was a very walkable country, Alex told them. So much so that hikers and outdoor enthusiasts flocked to its pastures, mountains, and beaches.

There were churches and mosques and temples at every turn. The people coming and going were every shade of the human rainbow. Some were covered from head to toe in bright fabric. Others were nearly bare in strips of fabric that left only a little to the imagination.

"It's like a utopia," said Esme. But she had to amend her statement when they pulled up to the palace. "No, it's paradise."

The castle was built into the side of a mountain. It looked like a small city that sprang from the earth. The stone looked more golden than like actual brick. The spires sparkled as they reached up toward the sky. Lush green foliage sprouted between some of the buildings furthering the notion that the castle had sprung fully formed from the ground.

"That's why the clouds moved in on what had previously been a fine day."

They looked up to see a man, who could only be described as dashing, coming down the steps of the castle. His skin was honey gold. His hair jet black. His huge, almond-shaped eyes were blue. His accent was somewhere at the center of a Venn diagram of British, French, and Spanish.

"Oh, who let the refuse in here," Alex groaned. But he smiled as he did so. He took two steps at a time until the two men met in the middle. Once forearms were clasped, they continued on with a complicated handshake, and then the two embraced. "Zhi, it's good to see you."

"Your highness." Zhi came down the steps and bowed to Penelope.

"Hello, Duke Mondego," said the little princess. "I should warn you. Uncle Alex flew in a chef to win the baking competition, and she's very good."

The man's blue eyes landed on Esme. "Oh, no. It's not me."

Beside Esme, Jan gave a little wave.

"Well," said the duke, as he looked Jan up and down, "if her cooking is as lovely as her face, then I'm toast." He reached for and kissed Jan's hand.

But before Zhi's lips could make contact with Jan's palm, Alex swatted them apart. "None of that. Don't let him get into your head."

"I would do no such thing," said the duke. "And because my sworn frenemy here doesn't possess the manners to introduce us properly, may you allow me to present myself. I am Diego Zhi Wen den Bernadino, the Duke of Mondego."

"Wow, that's a mouthful. I'm Jan." Jan pressed her hand to her chest. "Jan Peppers of Jersey City. Um, may I present my friend; Esmeralda Pickett of Long Island."

The Duke reached for and kissed Esme's hand. Thankfully, Alex didn't swat them apart. When Zhi's lips touched Esme's skin, she felt a hint of warmth, but not a tingle. Definitely no sparklers.

"Low blow putting someone in the kitchen as beautiful as this, your highness."

A lesser woman would've blushed and batted her eyelashes at the praise. Jan was not a lesser woman. If Esme knew her best friend well, and she did, she knew Jan would think the reference to her looks instead of her culinary skill was an insult.

"Well, it just so happens I've hired a ringer myself," Zhi continued when he didn't get the response he was looking for from Jan. "A certain James Beard award winner."

Alex snorted. "Which is why you'll lose. Again."

"I suppose Chef Peppers is a fusion foodinista?"

"She's a sorceress with spices."

"Well, I can't wait to give your food a try." Zhi winked at Jan, but still got her game face. He frowned and turned back to Alex, who was smiling with glee at his friend's failure to entice his chef. "In the meantime, I hear wedding bells may be heard soon?"

Jan and Esme looked to Alex.

Alex's smug grin dropped, and his hands went up as though a fire sprang to life before him. "Oh, no. Not me. He's talking about my brother."

That knocked the wind out of Esme. "Leo's engaged?"

"Not yet," said Alex. "But he is looking."

"King Leo needs to have a male heir," said the duke. "Or our wayward prince here will take the throne when he kicks on, heaven forbid."

"You're next in line after me," said Alex.

"Egad," said the duke. "We all know that Pen is best suited for the job."

Penelope, who was leaning into Esme's side nodded in agreement. The little girl was likely tired from all the day's activity and needed a nap.

"Speaking of the Pea," said Alex, swooping Penelope up into his arms and rallying her, "we need to get her inside before she turns into a pumpkin."

"Uncle Alex, that's make believe. And it was a carriage that turns into a pumpkin."

"I thought you said you didn't read fairytales," said Esme.

Penelope shrugged. "They're hard to avoid. I may have glanced at one or two."

Alex deposited the three girls in the capable hands of the Head of Housekeeping, Mrs. Dolevitt. The woman had a warm smile and a crown of fluffy white hair that bounced as she walked. She sent Penelope up with a maid and then turned her attention to Esme and Jan.

As Mrs. Dolevitt led them down the hall of the old castle, Esme kept stopping and touching and looking and even sniffing things like a curious little puppy. The housekeeper was tolerant. She appeared to love the castle as much as Esme was falling in love with it.

"How long have you worked here?" asked Esme.

"My whole life. My mother worked here before I did, and her mother and grandmother before her. We are the longest serving family in the castle."

"You're practically royalty yourself," said Esme.

"The only throne I've sat on is a porcelain one." The older woman laughed. She looked to be of middle eastern descent. Somewhere between Spain and the tip of Africa, but to Esme's ears, she rolled her R's like a French woman.

Esme stopped again when they passed a statue of a warrior with his sword drawn in preparation to face whatever monster might come his way. Just then, a low moan sounded from the walls. Logically, Esme knew it was likely pipes, but to her imagination, it sounded like a dragon preparing to attack.

"Careful, dear," said Mrs. Dolevitt. "There are a lot of repairs going on in preparation for the gala, so please excuse the mess and the noise."

As if on cue, the groaning noise sounded through the walls, practically vibrating the floor. Though she knew there were truly no such things as dragons, Esme's imagination was already running away with her. What if there was a beast in the belly of the dungeons? Or a griffin on the roof. Would Leo come down from his throne and rescue her? Would she even see him again this weekend in this massive place with all these people?

"I'm so sorry, my dears, but we weren't expecting you. Typical of Prince Alexander. I'm afraid we're quite full. All fifty royal guest bedrooms are taken."

"There're over fifty rooms in the castle?" said Jan.

"There are over five hundred rooms. Ten state rooms, forty offices, seventy bathrooms, one hundred staff bedrooms. And there are two ballrooms."

"You never have to leave," Esme sighed.

"In the early centuries, the queens of Cordoba never did," said Mrs. Dolevitt. "Women are treasured in this country, protected."

"What was the last queen like?" asked Esme.

"Queen Isabel was a good woman. Smart. Very beautiful. And kind. She took her duties seriously. She had many charitable endeavors. She and the king tried for many years to have children before being blessed with the princess. The queen's greatest sorrow was not giving the kingdom an heir before she passed away."

"Were they in love? King Leo and Queen Isabel?"

Mrs. Dolevitt frowned as though she hadn't understood the question. "It doesn't work like that with royalty. Their marriage was arranged when they were children. They got on well. I never saw them argue. King Leo consulted her often on decisions, very modern of him. He grieved when she passed. But it's time he remarries."

"I suppose that will be arranged?" Esme asked.

"King Leo will do his own choosing this time."

Finally, they reached their destination. Mrs. Dolevitt turned the lock on an ancient looking door. "This is the old nursery. It hasn't been used since King Leo and Prince Alex were little ones."

Though it may not have been in use for years, a ruckus sounded from the adjoining room.

"Sorry," said Mrs. Dolevitt. "Some of the royal guests are using the other room as a day care."

"Are the children unattended?" Esme asked going over to the adjoining door. Before Mrs. Dolevitt could answer, Esme had already pulled the door open. It wasn't exactly chaos on the other side. Just disorganized confusion.

Candies and chips were set up on a table. Juice boxes were lined up like soldiers, a few boxes had spilled onto the floor. The kids were running around and squealing as though they'd been let loose for the first time in their lives.

"There are no nannies or governesses on the property," said Mrs. Dolevitt. "Princess Penelope has only tutors. The child is quite happy to spend much of her days sitting in her father's office while he works. She's never needed much looking after. She prefers to learn all day."

Esme spied Penelope sitting in a corner with a book as the chaos ensued around her. Jan turned back into the room. Kids weren't the baker's forte. But Esme was in her element. Esme took a step into the nursery.

There were five children gathered in the room including Penelope. They were a United Color of Benetton ad with skin hues that circled the globe. Esme supposed that was because this country was so diverse.

"Did you hear that?" Esme said loud enough over the din of noise. All young eyes looked up at her. Penelope put down her book. "I think a dragon is trying to enter the castle."

"There's no such thing as dragons," said a little boy with jet black hair and eyes just as dark.

As if on cue the clanging sound of pipes rattled the room. The children gasped and looked about.

Esme pursed her lips and shrugged. "If you say so." She turned to go back into her room. The clanking sounded again.

"Oh, no," a second boy exclaimed. His green eyes went wide as he looked at the walls. "There's a dragon in the walls. What do we do?"

"Tell our parents," said a blonde-haired girl that was about Penelope's age.

"No need to bother them," Esme replied. "Adults can't see or hear dragons. Only kids can."

"But you hear it," said the dark-haired boy.

"Because I'm around kids all day," said Esme. "So, I have special powers."

"Who are you?" asked the green-eyed boy.

"She's the kindergarten teacher from America," Penelope offered, as though announcing Esme at a grand ball.

"A kindergarten teacher?" said the dark-haired boy. "What's that?"

"It's an American type of teacher," Penelope answered.

"I have tutors," announced the boy with the green eyes. "I've never met one."

"You're from America?" asked the blonde-haired girl. "Where the streets are gold?"

Esme nodded. "Dragons love gold, which is why I know so much about them. I've come here undercover as a baker's assistant. But my true job is a dragon hunter. Isn't that right, your highness?"

Esme wasn't sure if Penelope would play along. To her surprise, the little princess put down her book and nodded.

"Perhaps the dragon is in the dungeons?" said Penelope.

"Perha-wait?" Esme jerked to attention. "You have real, live dungeons here?"

Penelope nodded enthusiastically. "Down at the bottom of the castle. It's a ways away."

Perfect. All part of Esme's master plan. "Take the lead, your royal highness. We're going dragon hunting."

CHAPTER NINETEEN

A king's work was never done. After his trip abroad to strengthen diplomatic relationships and brag a bit about his country's successes, Leo hit the ground running back on his home turf. Or rather, he hit the ground shoveling.

Groundbreaking and ribbon cutting were mainstays of his job. He shoveled already-loosened soil at a groundbreaking for a new, state-of-the-art retirement home for veterans. He snipped the ribbon at the entryway to a new wing named in his late wife's honor at a recreational center for underprivileged kids. He attended a luncheon hosted by two land barons whose families first discovered there was oil off the coast of Cordoba. He stopped briefly at an agricultural show and waved. He drove by the new railway station opening that would connect the east side of the country with the northwest, and he waved.

Before heading back to the palace, he stopped at the House of Commons and took tea with the Prime Minister. Cordoba had a House of Commons, where officials were elected, and a House of Lords, where lords were all men and women of titles. Unlike in the British Parliament, the Lords were all hereditary. But the two houses had to work together in order to implement new laws.

The current Prime Minister was a working-class young man who'd made his fortune in technology. Leo admired him greatly and often chose to sit with him and not speak a word of politics. This was one of those days. Once he'd reached the bottom of his tea cup, Leo said his goodbyes to the Prime Minister and hopped into his town car to head for home.

It had been a grueling day. Leo was looking forward to resting his voice and his facial muscles from all the smiling, folding his hands in his lap and letting them rest from all the waving, and closing his eyes where he could lose himself in a daydream of damsels and dragons and sweet cookies. Unfortunately, those dreams would have to wait.

"You know for someone supported by taxes and a massive family fortune from centuries of hoarding, you are the hardest working man I know."

"Where is security when you need it," moaned Leo.

His grin resurfaced, he reached out his hand and clasped his palm to his oldest friend, Omar, the Marquis of Navarre.

"I saw the car and decided to catch a ride to tonight's state dinner," said Omar. He brushed some stray strands out of his eyes. His dark hair and sunburned coloring made the man look more like a desert sheik who'd been dropped into western civilization.

"I thought you were out of the country on business?"

Omar was one of the hottest entertainment producers in Europe. He didn't need to work. He just loved the job.

"Just got back last night. Wouldn't miss Union Day.

Besides, it seems the most interesting drama is going on on our home front. I hear you met a special lady in the States."

Leo did close his eyes. And there was her face. Round like a heart. Huge brown eyes shining back at him. A smile he ached to taste, but already knew it would be sweeter than the cookies she baked him.

He could deny it, but Daniel and Omar had always been able to see right through him. Leo slumped back in his seat and sighed. "It's impossible."

"She said no?"

"No. I can't say yes. Even though I've never felt this way before. We are royals. We aren't made to feel all these emotions and butterflies." He sat forward, waving his hands in agitation. "You know, I always thought that was just a silly expression."

"Having feelings?"

"What? No, the butterflies in your stomach. It's real. There is something fluttering in my stomach. And I see stars, and I'm spouting poetry. But she's all wrong for me. She lives in a fairytale world where princes come to the rescue. I'm a king with real responsibilities. She wouldn't fit in my world. The partnership would benefit no one. She has no connections."

"Why do I get the feeling we're not talking about Lady Teresa of Almodovar?"

Omar leaned against the opposite car door and regarded Leo. Leo turned away from his friend. His hand rubbed at the back of his neck, then it scrubbed over his face. But he couldn't hide from his friend.

"I never thought I'd see the day," the marquis said. "You're smitten."

"Why do people keep saying that?"

"Saying what? That you're smitten?"

"No, that they never believed I could be. That I never could ..." He let the sentence trail off. He couldn't say he'd fallen in love. That was too far. "It's like my closest friends see me as some cold automaton."

"Because you are a cold automaton in this aspect of your life. It's always been duty first with you, even when we were children. I assumed your heart was mechanical, running on the fumes of your conquering ancestors. But, look," Omar leaned forward, opening his eyes with wide with exaggerated disbelief, "you're a real boy after all."

Leo reached over and punched his friend in the shoulder.

Omar only laughed at the jab. He knew he'd struck home. "Who is this Geppetto?"

Leo clenched his lips tight. He couldn't speak her name, or else the butterflies would be set loose into the world.

"She must be a new and recent addition to our circle," Omar began to deduce. "But you said she had no connections? A commoner?"

Leo looked out the window. It was the only way he could think to give away nothing to his friend who saw everything, more than he ever let on. An automaton?

Leo had intended to ignore his friend for the remainder of the car ride. Luckily, when he looked out the window, he saw they were pulling through the gates of the palace. As they angled around back, Leo saw that there was some kind of commotion in the gardens.

A small crowd had gathered. There were mainly children, a few staff members, and other adults. They all stood around the decapitated head of what once was a stone dragon statue.

"What's this?" Leo asked as he approached the group. His feet stopped when Esme broke from the crowd.

He'd had every intention of avoiding her over the next few days. He hadn't even made it past the first day. Her hair was loose. Her cheeks were flushed. Her eyes were bright. Set against the backdrop of his green gardens she looked every bit the picture of a damsel in distress.

"It's my fault," said Esme. "We were playing a game, and it got a little out of hand."

"I thought it was a real dragon," said the dark-haired boy. He was the Viscount of Jucar's son. "I tried to slay it. I was trying to save the gala."

Esme got down and hugged the child who was close to tears. "You were a brave and valiant knight."

"He's no knight. He's a future viscount." The child's father pulled his boy away and glared between his heir and Esme. "It was reckless and unbecoming of one of nobility."

"He's just a child," said Esme.

"No, you little chit. He's of noble blood, and he can't behave in such a way. You'll do well to not speak so forwardly to your betters."

"That's enough," said Leo, his tired voice boomed loud enough to be heard in the turrets. "I'll have you know, Jucar, that Ms. Picket is an honored guest of mine."

Jucar's molars ground. His eyes cast down from his king, but they still burned a hole straight through Esme. He bowed his head to Leo. "We'll pay for the damage, of course."

"No," said Esme. "It was my fault. I'll pay for it."

"No one's paying for anything," said Leo. "It was already in need of repair. I'll take care of it. Everyone can go back to their business or their play."

The Viscount practically cuffed his son as he stormed off. The staff pretended not to see as they dispersed. The other children trailed off, including Penelope. She gave a sad smile of regret to her father, and Leo's heart twisted. Whatever joy had been in her eyes, in all the children's eyes, was now gone after the display. Esme watched the scene with a cloud hovering over her beautiful face.

"I'm so sorry," she said. "I was just trying to have some fun with them. They were cooped up inside, and I figured I could get some of that energy out before bedtime."

Every fiber of his being urged him to go to her and take her in his arms, to tell her that she'd had good intentions. But good intentions weren't enough in this realm. "You just have to realize this isn't a fairytale, Esme. It's the real world."

She looked up at him then. Though there was a cloud of sadness over her, her eyes were as bright and hopeful as ever. Not a dragon truck, nor a decapitated stone dragon would ever deter this woman.

"I still believe there's magic in ordinary things," said Esme.

"So you slay a priceless dragon statue given to my family over a century ago?"

"A century ago? That sounds like it would be expensive."

Leo nodded, and she cringed. The way her nose scrunched and her lips pursed made the butterflies in his stomach turn into raging wasps. They were desperate to get out, to get to her for a taste of what they knew was honey on those lips.

"Oh, Leo. I'm so sorry. You have to let me make up for it."

"How? Should I lock you in a tower and throw away the key for a hundred years?"

She lifted one shoulder and tilted her head in a way that told him she was seriously considering it. So was he.

"There are worse fates," she said.

That didn't sound like an ill-fated idea at all. Keeping

her captive sounded like the best idea he'd heard all day, all year, all his life.

A throat cleared behind Leo. Leo glanced over his shoulder and was startled to find Omar still standing there.

Leo cleared his own throat. He straightened his jacket, running his hands over his torso in a physical attempt to quiet the raging in his belly. "Just try to stay out of trouble, Ms. Pickett."

"No more dragon hunts." She put her right hand to her forehead and saluted. "You got it, your majesty."

With a nod, Leo turned on his heel and headed inside. The silence from the marquis was deafening.

"What?" Leo growled when they were a distance away from Esme.

"Nothing," said Omar.

"Right, it's nothing."

"Sure thing, Pinocchio."

CHAPTER TWENTY

Unlike Esme, Jan spent the afternoon testing the local cuisine with Prince Alex. She'd come back smelling of exotic spices and wearing a huge grin on her characteristically serious face. The two friends were in one of the three kitchens of the castle when Mrs. Dolevitt happened upon them with the head chef in tow.

The man in the pristine white apron had blinked and rubbed his eyes when he saw that the delectable smell was coming from the machinations of a female chef. More and more, Esme was learning that certain parts of this enchanted kingdom were still in the dark ages when it came to women's equality.

But, as the saying goes, a way to a man's heart was through his stomach. So, after a taste test, the chef invited Jan up to the big kitchen to help with the dessert for tonight's state dinner. Esme tagged along, hoping to catch a glimpse of a certain royal.

"We'll mix a little cumin and cinnamon, with a dash of cayenne," said Jan, tossing in a couple of pinches and a dash of the spices.

"That's new," said Esme. "Sweet and spicy all in one dessert pie. This place has broadened your imagination."

A secret smile spread across Jan's face. Esme had noticed a definite pep to her friend's step as she moved about the huge kitchen. She knew it had to be more than the stainless steel appliances. Jan had worked at high-end restaurants before.

"Or maybe a certain someone has broadened your imagination? Maybe a certain prince?"

The smile dissolved from the pie maker's face like the spices melting into the mixture. Jan's head jerked up and looked around at the staff, but no one paid them any attention. "Stop it. He's a prince. I'm from Jersey."

"It's possible."

Jan sat down her mixing spoon and dusted the flour off her hands. "Esme, I say this because I love you; Girl, pull your head out of the clouds."

Esme crossed her arms over her chest and leaned her hip against the counter as she regarded her friend.

"We're here in this world for a visit, not a mortgage. Girls like us don't stay in a fairyland world. And before you bring up Kate and Meghan," Jan held up her index finger before Esme could get in a word, "just remember that took years of strife to change that monarchy. There were bumps, broken hearts, and crashes along the way. This kingdom is still practicing ancient traditions. Do you want to be a bump?"

She wasn't going to be a bump. And even if this road she was on with Leo was rocky, she knew it was worth it for one good reason. "There's a thing between Leo and me."

"I get it. I see it," said Jan.

Jan's confirmation of the thing pleased Esme more than she could say. That unnamable thing grew in her heart at being acknowledged.

"But it's just a thing," Jan continued. "It's not even named."

Of course, it wasn't named. But it would be. Soon. She and Leo just needed to spend more time together to define what was happening between them.

Jan came to stand before her, looking Esme directly in the eye. "You're a smart girl. Don't risk your heart on anything but a proper noun."

Part of Esme knew Jan had a point. Both women had faced their fair share of disappointments at the hands of the opposite sex. But Leo was different.

"Esme, you're not even invited to dinner. Cinderella was at least invited to the ball."

"I'm helping my mean BFF prepare dessert in the kitchen."

"Your BFF, who loves you because you're the rock in her world. See, that; love and rock. Those are both nouns you can stand on."

Esme didn't want to argue with Jan. Unlike her bestie, Esme still believed love was real. She still wanted it in her life. And right now, there was only one man she could see herself offering that word, which could be both a verb and a noun, to.

She wanted to love Leo. She wanted to be loved by Leo. She wanted to be Leo's love, and him hers.

"Smells lovely." Mrs. Dolevitt came through the kitchen doors that lead to the dining area.

Esme craned her neck, but she couldn't see anything. She did hear the clinking of glasses and the low murmur of conversation. There was a belly laugh, but she didn't think it was Leo's. He had a light chuckle that was more of a delighted smile with a gush of breath than anything.

"How are things going at the state dinner?" Esme asked.

"Very well. Mainly because the parents are all relaxed due to all their children being sound asleep from running about today."

Esme would pat herself on the back, but Mrs. Dolevitt did it for her.

"You wouldn't happen to be looking for a job as a palace governess, now would you?" asked the housekeeper.

Esme cocked her head as though to ponder the thought. It wasn't beyond the realm of consideration. Especially if she'd leave behind Principal Clark for King Leonidas.

"There is one child who is still awake." Mrs. Dolevitt inclined her head to the door behind Esme.

Esme turned and found Penelope standing in the doorway, she wasn't as bright eyed and bushy tailed as she'd left her a couple hours ago. The child looked tired and was putting up a fight against sleep. Esme wondered if anyone had ever needed to tell the child no for any reason. She was always so well behaved.

"You said I could help with the baking?" Penelope said. "To practice my fractions."

Not only was the child well behaved and well mannered, her requests were also always to increase her academic prowess. Really? Where did this creature come from?

"I'm afraid we're all done with the fractions tonight, your highness," said Jan. "But I could definitely use your help tomorrow. You can be in charge of all the measuring. I hear you're good with flour."

Penelope giggled and then stifled a yawn.

"Princess Penelope," said Esme. "I've seen a lot of this castle, but I haven't seen your room. Would you show me?"

The girl's eyes glittered awake as she nodded. She reached out her hand, and Esme took the girl's small one in her own.

By the time they'd reached the grand staircase, the little princess was leaning into Esme, and her steps slowed. Esme reached down and lifted the five-year-old up and carried her up the grand staircase.

She expected a frilly room, but the princess' room was tasteful in soft, muted colors. A picture of a woman hung on the wall. The Queen.

She was very beautiful. She didn't grin. Instead, there was a small, dignified smile on Queen Isabel's face and a softness to her eyes. Esme had imagined the woman harsh and stern, but that's not what she saw at all in the portrait.

"I don't remember her much," Penelope said from the cradle of Esme's arms. "My memories are fading."

"But can you still feel her?" asked Esme. "She's watching over you. She lives in your heart."

Esme helped Penelope as she undressed. Once in a plain nightgown, Penelope climbed under the covers and allowed Esme to tuck her into bed.

"I just remembered something," said Penelope. "My mother used to do this; tuck me in. And then my father would lean down and kiss my forehead. He still does that. Even if I'm sleeping."

"How do you know he does it if you're asleep?"

"I suppose I can feel him, you know, in my heart."

Esme leaned down and kissed the girl's forehead.

"Father will get remarried one day soon," said Penelope. "Do you think my new mother will tuck me in even though I'm not her daughter?"

"She won't be able to help it, Pea. You're so easy to love. I only just met you, and you're very dear to me."

"We'll always be friends, won't we, Esme?"

"Forever and after, sweet pea."

Penelope closed her eyes and slipped off into dream

land. Esme meant those words. The little girl had captured a piece of her heart. Adoration, it might be called. Attachment might be a better word.

Esme brushed the girl's hair from her forehead. In sleep, she finally looked her age. She wished the little princess dreams of a world that let her remain a child for as long as possible.

With one final kiss to wish her happy dreams, Esme rose to find the king standing in the doorway.

CHAPTER TWENTY-ONE

"We need to direct more funds to infrastructure."

"Only if it's for high speed internet and other technologies. Cordoba is far too behind in this area of innovation."

"The oil in our waters is all we need to focus on. That is our main source of wealth."

"But it needs to be done with more care for the environment. Right, your majesty?"

Leo clenched his hands so as not to work the nerve pulsing in his temple. For the past hour, he'd been fielding questions and breaking up disputes. Though no children were at this dinner, he felt like the only adult in the room of squabbling adolescents. It was always this way when the House of Lords broke bread with the House of Commons. The problem was, this wasn't a parliamentary meeting. There were foreign dignitaries at the table, and a family argument had broken off around the dinner table.

He'd had less than thirty minutes to rest his aching jaw

before he had to plaster on that noble half-smile again. Luckily, there were no scissors, shovels, or other items that could be used as blunt weapons at the table.

"I say this is a state dinner and not the parliamentary floor," said Leo. "Why not table this argument now that dessert is being placed before us."

The country's leadership let out a collective, disgruntled sigh, but when the pie was put before them, they dug in. For glorious moments, mouths were filled with sweet and savory treats instead of arguments. Leo waved his slice away. He'd had enough to chew on for today.

"Just try a bite," Alex coaxed from his spot on Leo's right. "It's like tasting heaven. Jan and Esme worked all evening on it."

At the mention of Esme's name, Leo waved the server back over. Just one bite wouldn't hurt. Of course, he was wrong.

Just one taste of the pie brought the kindergarten teacher clearly into focus in his mind. The pastry was sweet and airy but also complex and layered. He went back for a second bite.

"I hear wedding bells are in your future," said the Prime Minister from his spot on Leo's left.

All clattering of silverware, all conversation, all chewing came to an immediate halt. All eyes cast downward as though no one wanted him to know they were eavesdropping. Leo took a moment to swallow the last morsel of his second helping.

"Of course, we hoped for a Cordovian pairing," said the Viscount of Jucar. "But a Spanish duchess will suffice, I suppose."

"Especially one in the maritime industry," said the Prime Minister. "The union will create jobs for our citizens."

"All well and good for Cordoba," said Daniel who was seated a few chairs down from Leo. "But what about his majesty's heart?"

Now heads did raise. Not only heads but eyebrows. Everyone looked around as though they weren't sure what the earl's punch line was.

"My heart is upstairs," said Leo. "If you'll excuse me, I'm going to take a moment to say goodnight to my daughter."

He made his way out of the dining room. He knew his country had a stake in what he did in his personal life, but he was not going to discuss it around the dinner table as though it were a parliamentary procedure. He was going to do the right thing. He always did the right thing. It was in his breeding.

He knew in his head that he was doing the right thing by considering marriage to Lady Teresa. He knew it was the best thing for Cordoba's future both as a monarchy and as an industrial state.

His head was very clear on those facts. So, why was his heart thumping a different tune? And why was his head paying attention to the beat?

It pounded in his chest, begging for his full attention. It had never beat so loud or so clear in his life. At least he supposed it hadn't. He was a logical man and always trusted his intuition and deductive skills. But Leo couldn't remember a time when he'd listened to his own heart.

Arriving at Penelope's door, he heard voices. He knew she was there before he opened the door. He felt her before he saw her. That sweet and savory smell of hers knocked him back when he cracked the door open.

"My mother used to do this; tuck me in. And then my father would lean down and kiss my forehead. He still does that. Even if I'm sleeping."

"How do you know he does it if you're asleep?"

"I suppose I can feel him, you know, in my heart."

Esme leaned down and kissed his little girl's forehead. Leo remained stock still in the doorway, looming like some great beast as her delicate finger lovingly caressed his child's features.

"Father will get remarried one day soon," said Penelope. "Do you think my new mother will tuck me in even though I'm not her daughter?"

"She won't be able to help it, Pea. You're so easy to love. I only just met you, and you're very dear to me."

"We'll always be friends, won't we Esme?"

"Forever and after, sweet pea."

Penelope closed her eyes and slipped off into dream land. Esme planted another kiss to the child's forehead. She leaned over and stared at Penelope for a few moments longer as though she were saying a prayer or casting a benevolent spell like a fairy godmother.

Wow. Now she had him doing it; believing in fairytales. Him, the no-nonsense, by-the-book, country-before-heart king of this realm was off in Lala Land.

Esme froze when she saw him. But in that same instance, she smiled at him. The fireworks in his head were now bombs being shot from his neurotransmitters. The blasts cleared every thought from his head, and his heart raced to take the lead.

"Good evening, your majesty."

She curtsied. Well, her approximation of a curtsey. It was more of a bending bob. She straightened and looked at him expectantly. Whether for him to remark on her manners or to respond in kind, he wasn't sure. Leo was too busy fighting the war raging inside him, and he was losing.

He stepped inside the room and shut the door behind him with a snick of the lock.

"Penelope wanted to help with the pie making," said Esme. "As you know, fractions are her jam. But she probably stayed up past her bedtime after traveling and all the day's excitement. She'll sleep well like the other children."

The battle inside Leo ceased for a split second. He bent over his daughter's reposed form and pressed his lips to Penelope's forehead. It was the same spot Esme had pressed her lips. Leo caught Esme's sweetness in his nose, then on his lower lip. He tugged that corner of his lip inside his mouth, and something clicked inside him.

"How was dinner?" she asked. "How are you? You're probably exhausted too. You've been going all day."

Leo reached to the panel on the wall and turned out the light. Esme's form was illuminated in the moonlight, clear as day, like a living fairy from another world. He stalked towards her, pushing her deeper into the room.

Esme backed up at his advance, but he knew she wasn't frightened. Though she should be as Leo stalked her like prey. They wound up out on the balcony where he closed that door with another quiet snick. The sounds of victory beat out in his heart. The canon fire of his brain ceased, and all was quiet except for Esme's shallow breaths.

"Leo?"

Just one taste. Just once. That wouldn't hurt.

He took another step. Esme stopped retreating. She held her ground.

Tilting her head back, she gazed up into his eyes. His intentions had to be clear on his face. He couldn't fight it anymore. When the realization of the inevitable dawned on her, Esme gasped. Leo took advantage of her parted lips.

It was such a simple gesture, a kiss. Just a press of the lips. He'd always found the alignment of the two heads tricky. Head on would cause noses to bump. So one person would have to tilt to the left and the other to the right. The coordination was the key, but he'd never figured out how to communicate which direction he would descend to let his partner know so that she might go the opposite direction.

Without words, he and Esme were in perfect synch. She went left, and he went right. Their lips met in the middle in perfect alignment.

Off in the distance fireworks went off igniting the night's sky. Realistically, Leo knew that the pyrotechnics were in preparation for tomorrow's Union Day celebration. But, for the first time in his life, he let his imagination run.

His kiss with Esme had set the world on fire. It certainly set him on fire. Every good sense in his brain burned to cinders at the touch of her lips to his. The sweet taste of her washed all reason from him. He felt full and starving at the same time.

One taste would not do. Somewhere inside his short circuiting brain, he'd known that would be the case. He pressed into her and deepened the kiss.

It might be their second kiss, but it was the one and only time that he would taste her. He had to make it last. And so he took one more before breaking away from her.

It was the fight of a lifetime tearing his lips from hers. His lips won, but his arms were still on the battlefield, wrapped tightly around Esme's torso, holding her close. He rested his forehead against hers continuing to breathe in her sweet scent.

He'd only kissed two other women in his lifetime, and it had been nothing like what had just happened between him and Esme.

"That was the most selfish thing I've ever done in my life," he said.

"You did it spectacularly well," she said. "But, as a teacher, I know that practice makes perfect."

Her hand reached up and cupped his chin. Her lips were about to land the deathblow to his shattered sense of duty if he didn't do something. He didn't want to do anything but let her claim her victory. Somehow, Leo found the will power to turn his head.

"I'm sorry," he said. "I can't. I have to get married."

"Before you kiss me again?" She grinned up at him with pure joy in her eyes.

His heart stopped at the look. He knew then that she would say yes if he asked. Leo wanted nothing more in this world than to ask that question of her. Instead, he had to crush her dreams.

"To a future duchess," he said.

The first crack was tiny. It was a single wrinkle in her brow of confusion. Despite her wild imagination, Esme was a very smart woman. Within a few seconds, reality dawned on her.

"I don't think there's a degree in becoming a duchess, is there?" she asked.

He wanted to laugh. She was still making jokes in the face of despair. But this predicament they were in now in was far too tragic for humor.

She withdrew her hand from his cheek leaving Leo feeling cold and alone. "No, I suppose you need someone born a duchess. And now I'm coming to understand the selfish part of your statement."

She took a single step away from him, and Leo felt bereft like he was deserted on an island. "Esme, I'm so sorry."

She gave him her back and leaned against the railing.

Her shoulders caved, and her head bowed as though she were going to be sick. "You're going to marry someone else?"

He nodded. Then realized she couldn't see him. "Yes."

But his voice sounded like the croak of a frog. He'd been a king, but when the woman of his dreams kissed him, he turned into a frog. Wasn't that irony?

Esme turned back to him. Her features were scrunched in confusion. "Truly?"

Leo tilted his head back and looked at the sky. There were no answers there. No dragons came to swoop them both away into a fairytale world where they could be together. Reality was closing in on all sides.

"But we have a thing," she said.

He looked back at her. "A thing?"

"Yes. Between us." She motioned with her hand at the empty space between them. "There's a thing."

"What thing?"

Now she threw her hands up. "I don't know. It's unnamed. But it's there. You know it's there. It's butterflies in your stomach. It's fireflies in your head. It's sparklers in your heart."

Oh, *that* thing. The thing he'd imagined for the past couple of days. The thing that was all too real but could never survive in the harsh reality they found themselves in.

"Yes, I know what you mean," was all he could manage.

"So, you can't marry someone else."

"I have to."

"Have to?"

It was such a simple question. But the answer was so complex. "I must produce a male heir for Cordoba. My wife has to be of noble blood."

"Has to?"

He huffed in frustration. "This is just the way things are. I can't change it."

"Why not? You're the king."

Leo opened his mouth. Then closed it. He had no words for her.

"Why did you kiss me? You were, what? Sowing your royal oats with a commoner?"

He reached out and grabbed her forearm. He wanted to shake her for saying such a thing. "You're more than that to me."

"Yeah, *I* know." She stared him down, her brown gaze accusatory and unapologetic. "Do *you*?"

He knew he had to let her go. Instead, he cupped both her shoulders with his hands. "Esmeralda Pickett, you are the most magical thing that's ever happened to me. I kissed you because I just wanted, for one moment in my life, something for me, something I dreamed of, my own fairytale."

She nodded as though that made sense. "But now you're going to push me back into the real world? Do you think any man is ever going to live up to you?"

He hated the idea of Esme and another man. "Esme, I would give anything for things to be different."

"No, you wouldn't." She broke from his embrace and stepped beyond his reach. "You have everything. And what you don't have, you can get. You're a king, Leo. Change the rules."

"It's not that simple."

She shook her head at him reminding him of every teacher he'd ever disappointed with a low grade or work below the standard they held him to. Instead of another reprimand, Esme turned on her heel and headed for the door.

"Where are you going?" he called out to her.

"Back to reality," she said. "Right now, that's on the other side of the castle, just above the servants' quarter, on the other side of the nursery. Come find me when you come to your senses."

CHAPTER TWENTY-TWO

She was ruined. Esme understood how a kiss would ruin girls in the Victorian age. How being caught out on a balcony alone with a gentleman was grounds for instant matrimony. She wished she could suffer the consequences of marriage. To leg-shackle Leo into a wedding and have him kiss her like that every night and then on into the day and another taste at lunch.

But they hadn't been caught. Then she had walked away. And he hadn't come.

Not later that night. Not early the next morning. Not at all.

Because she wasn't good enough. Her blood wasn't royal blue. Just her shirt collar. Esme tugged at the collar of her blouse and dabbed the corner of her eyes with the fabric.

He'd taken just a taste of her, he said. Just a sip to know what it would be like. A morsel to savor in his mind for the rest of his life.

She should've been flattered after he'd uttered those words under the moonlight. But she was devastated and bereft in the bright light of a new day.

And teary. Her eyes burned. Her vision fogged. Her nose itched.

Was something burning?

In answer, the pan she had been minding went from smoking hot to engulfed in fire. Esme reached for the pan's handle. Luckily, before her bare hand could reach the metal, a mitten-clad hand swatted her away in the nick of time before she could add third-degree burns to the list of her complaints.

Jan tossed salt into the pan, ruining the mixture. Then she clamped a lid over top of it. "Esmeralda, why don't you take a break."

Jan never called Esme by her full first name unless she was exasperated. It was the day of the pie competition; the reason they were there. Esme was meant to be a help, but she was making a mess.

"No, I'm not abandoning you during your time of need," Esme insisted.

"You're not helping, sweetie. The way you're going, you'll burn the castle down."

Would a kitchen fire bring Leo down to this level of the castle? Perhaps he'd come to her rescue again if she destroyed a wing of his home. But no, she couldn't add arson to her list of failings. And so, she took off her apron and headed out of the kitchens.

But once outside the kitchens, she didn't know which way to turn. Esme looked up at the vaulted ceilings of the palatial estate. For the first time since her stay, she noticed the cracked paint on the walls, a few tiles were missing here and there, and the draft along the corridor told her that new windows would be a welcome addition.

The facade of the castle was the stuff of dreams, but she wanted the reality. She didn't want to be secluded in a high tower. She didn't want to be a damsel in distress. She wanted to pick up a sword and go and charge ahead and take back her king.

This tale didn't need a hero. It needed a heroine. Leo was the one being forced into a marriage he didn't want because of duty. But that's not how the fairytales went.

Esme marched up to the first group of people she saw. They were dressed in the uniforms of the maid staff. "Excuse me? Would you happen to know where the king is at this moment?"

"Likely in his office, ma'am."

Esme nodded. "And which way is that?"

"East wing, second floor." The maid pointed.

Esme picked up her feet and marched on. Determination in her strides. Dragons guarded treasure. Witches cast spells. Parents imposed harsh rules. Knights in shining armor came to the rescue. In this story, Esme would come to the rescue. She knew enough stories to make this work.

The trek to the east wing was long. Once there, she faced her first obstacle. Instead of dragons or witches, there stood a single guard at the door of Leo's office.

"I'm sorry, ma'am," he said. "You can't go in there."

"I just need a word with the king," she said.

"Do you have an appointment?"

"No, but it's gravely important."

The man looked unmoved.

"If you just tell him it's Esme. Esmeralda Pickett."

The man did not move. But the door did open. Inside, Esme caught a glimpse of Leo. He held an old fashion corded phone to his ear with his shoulder. With one hand, he flipped through documents. With the other hand, he pinched the bridge of his nose.

He looked stressed and tense and unhappy. Esme took a step toward him, preparing to cross the threshold and get this rescue party started. Unfortunately, one of the bad guys blocked her way.

"Can I help you, Miss Pickett?"

Esme looked up at the imposing, immovable figure of Giles. His nose was pinched even more than normal, his gaze as sharp as glass.

"Giles, can I talk to Leo for just one second?"

"His majesty, King Leonidas," Giles emphasized each of Leo's titles, "is busy with matters of state at the moment."

Esme looked at the gap between Giles and the guard. She was thin enough to slip through them. As though they anticipated her next move, they closed the distance.

She wanted to stamp her foot. She wanted to shout to get Leo's attention. But she didn't. She knew that would show the true shade of her blue collared upbringing.

Giles took her by the arm and led her away from the door as it closed. "You might be a guest of the prince, but do not wear out our hospitality, Miss Pickett."

"What do you have against him being happy, Giles?"

"People's lives and livelihoods are at stake while you're caught in a world of make believe."

"He would choose to be with me if he had the chance."

"He had the chance. He could abdicate the throne. He didn't. Because he takes his very real duties seriously. Play time is over."

Giles showed her to a back door that led to the front of the castle. "Are you kicking me out?"

"I wish it were within my power. But as I said, you're a guest of the prince. However, you are hereby banned from the east wing of this castle. Trust me, it's for your own good. You don't want to embarrass yourself any further. Duty trumps everything with royalty. That's the job. You'd do well to learn that lesson."

But Esme was a teacher and not a student. She knew that particular instruction was the wrong answer. She walked through the gardens plotting her next attack on the beasts that guarded her fair king.

It would appear she wouldn't have to wait long. From a side door, she saw Leo emerge. He was surrounded by a number of other distinguished men, security, and Giles. Before Esme could decide the best way to get his attention, he ducked into the car and was gone.

She needed a way into the city. She couldn't ask Alex as he and Jan were preparing for the pie competition. Her salvation arrived in the form of a tour bus.

Camera toting and map unfolding tourists clamored off the bus for a look at the castle. Esme hopped on and waited for the bus to take her into town, certain that that was where Leo had gone. Unfortunately, twenty minutes later, she discovered that the tour bus wasn't headed to town. It was headed to the docks. Her rescue mission was thwarted once again.

But she wasn't done. She would not let him make a choice that would lead to unhappiness. She loved Leo too much for that.

Yes, that's what the thing was. It was a full blown case of love. It had taken root when she'd fallen onto his chest as he'd rescued her from a dragon truck. It had begun to grow when they'd battled flour fairies in a hotel suite kitchen. It had blossomed last night when his lips had met hers.

She was in love, and she was not giving up. She just had to get back to the castle and plot her next move. She had time as the tour bus wouldn't head back to the castle for another twenty minutes.

Esme took the time to walk along the pier. The waters around the island nation were pristine, which she found fascinating since there was oil in the depths. But Cordoba drilled responsibly. Of course, they did. Leo was their king, and he'd never let anyone get hurt on his watch.

She looked out at the most magnificent yacht she'd ever seen. It was gleaming white with gold trim, something fit for a king. It probably belonged to Leo.

Coming down the pier of the docked yacht was a woman who was as equally glamorous as the boat behind her. From her tailored skirt to her designer heels and the jewels around her neck which sparkled in the sunlight, she looked expensive.

She was also looking down at her phone and not up. She didn't see the trolley cart that had come loose and was headed her way on a slow stroll. Esme may have failed her first few tasks this morning, but she sprang into action once more.

The trolley crashed into the water just as Esme reached the woman and pulled her to the side. The woman looked from Esme's hand on her arm to the drops of water on the pier that had splashed up from the drowned cart.

"You just saved my life," said the woman.

"Well, maybe not your life, but definitely your shoes. I don't think leather would appreciate salty water."

The woman laughed. As she did, her head wiggled a bit, and a warm scent hit Esme's nose. This woman smelled of warm cinnamon apples, much like the poison pie Jan always made for Esme.

"Cell phones are the new villains," said Esme. "Distracting us from reality."

"They're also magic," said the woman. "Connecting people half a world away. I couldn't run my business empire without this thing." She caressed her phone to her chest as though she prized it more than her shoes or her gems.

"Are you in fashion?" Esme asked. "A model perhaps?"

"Gracious, no." She laughed again. "I take that as a compliment. But I'm in business, mostly maritime ventures."

"I don't suppose you're a modern day pirate, sailing the high seas on a luxury yacht?"

"In these heels?" she grinned. "No. But this is my ship. I designed it myself."

"It's gorgeous. I would pay good money to sail around this country. I've only seen it from the airplane and the highways. A cruise around the island would be magical. Like a Disney cruise with a royal theme because of the royal family here."

"A luxury cruise line?" The woman had been steadily tapping on her phone during the entire conversation, but her thumb paused, and she regarded Esme with full attention. "That's brilliant."

"Or a family cruise line. Children would love the castles. I hear you can see them from the coast."

"Even better. I'm going to present this to King Leo."

"You know the king?"

"Know him. If all goes according to plan, I'll be married to him by winter."

She said it so dryly that Esme thought she was joking. But this didn't look like the type of woman to joke about something so serious. Ruined designer shoes? Maybe. Marriage to a king? Not likely.

Esme stopped breathing. This was her rival? The evil duchess who would ruin Leo's life with an arranged marriage.

It couldn't be. This woman was beautiful and successful

and ... nice. Though a little preoccupied. And she came bearing gifts of business dealings. How was Esme going to compete with that?

"Ah, there's my knight in a luxury car now."

The same town car that Esme had seen pull off with Leo inside pulled up. Leo was the first to step out. He stopped in his tracks when he saw Esme.

CHAPTER TWENTY-THREE

*L*eo was exhausted. He hadn't slept a wink last night, not with the taste of Esme lingering on his lips. Not with the feel of her still resonating in his palms. Not with the smell of her forever imprinted on his brain. He had no idea how he would spend the rest of his life without another taste, another touch, another whiff of her sweetness.

He'd paced the halls of the east wing for a few hours. Somehow, after midnight, he ended up on the west wing just down the hall from the nursery. His steps halted there on the last step of the staircase.

He felt like a ghost haunting the castle; unable to rest with an unquiet need for human contact. Like any spirit unable to let go of their old life, Leo was having trouble moving on to the next chapter of his life.

So much so, that the next morning he mixed up the names of all his cabinet members. He spent five minutes speaking in French to the Japanese Prime Minister before the man politely interrupted him. Then he'd begun hallucinating.

While talking to a French member of Parliament, in French, about Cordovian wine, Leo could've sworn he saw Esme standing outside his office. When he'd gotten into the car later, he could've sworn he saw her standing by the beheaded dragon statue.

And now it was happening again.

He saw Esme standing beside Lady Teresa out on the pier. But, of course, it wasn't her. It was just his mind wishing it was her.

So why was Lady Teresa talking to the dream Esme as though she could see her too?

"Leo, darling, there you are."

Teresa leaned forward and kissed Leo on both sides of his cheeks. When Leo turned his head to receive a kiss on his left cheek, his gaze caught Esme's. It was the real Esme that stood before him.

He knew because he watched as the sparkles in her eyes dimmed. He watched the smile that had been on her beautiful face fade. He watched as her chin that had always been high and defiant, sank into her chest.

Leo's voice caught in his throat. The smell of warm cinnamon burnt his tongue and made his belly turn.

"I nearly lost my head a moment ago," Lady Teresa was saying. "This wonderful woman saved me. I'm sorry, what did you say your name was?"

"I didn't," said Esme, her voice barely above a whisper. "It doesn't matter."

"Do you need a ride?" asked Teresa. "It's the least I can do."

"No." She shook her head slowly. "I'd rather not intrude on ..."

Esme waved her hand between Leo and Teresa. She

didn't look at him. She wouldn't look at him. Her gaze turned faraway, well beyond his reach.

She was the ghost now. Just an apparition of her former, bright, spirited self. This vision of her would haunt Leo for the rest of his days.

"I'll call you a car," said Leo.

"No." Her tone was sharp. Her gaze lifted, pinning him with a glare that turned his heart into knots. "I'll find my own way."

It took everything for Leo to reach for Lady Teresa and not Esme. Even more will power for him to leave her standing on the pier. His gaze stayed fixed on the rear-view mirror until long after she was a dot on the horizon.

He watched her get farther and farther away from him. His hands clenched and unclenched until she was gone. It was truly over.

The tiredness hit him in full force. His head thumped back against the car seat. His every muscle ached and felt stiff at the same time. His throat felt like it was on fire.

"Leo? Did you hear me?"

He turned to Teresa. She regarded him with a quirk to her lip and a raise of her eyebrow. He had no idea what that expression meant? Was she angry with him? Amused by him?

If it had been Esme, he would've known that she was amused by his divided loyalties and would likely weave some imaginative tale to recapture his full attention. But Teresa wasn't Esme. He would have to get to know her quirks and eccentricities if she had any.

"How was your trip?" he asked.

"I got a lot accomplished," said Teresa, looking down at her phone instead of at him. "I closed a deal with the company that builds ships for the Royal Navy. I also managed to work on our deal."

Teresa was smart and ambitious. Leo's head knew those were great qualities for an addition to the country's government. This was why she was the best decision for Cordoba. But, in his heart, he couldn't help asking, was she the best decision for him?

"And I just got a great idea from that young woman back there," Teresa was saying.

"Esme?"

"Oh? Is that her name? You two know each other?"

"I ... We ... What was her idea?"

"A cruise line."

"A cruise line?"

"I'd initially thought of a luxury line when she brought it up. But she mentioned a family line, which is brilliant because most families are parents with children. And sometimes extended families. That multiplies the income. Brilliant."

"Yes, she is."

Leo had no idea what had brought Esme out to the waters that afternoon. She would likely call it fate.

It was fate that brought them together on the streets of New York. It was fate that had Penelope poke her head into Esme's class and then invite her to dinner. It was fate that Alex asked Esme's best friend to be his pie making champion this weekend. And now, again, it was fate that brought Esme face to face with the woman he'd intended to marry and put on the table an idea that could secure the future of his country.

"We can add it to our original plan," said Teresa. "I think the cruise line will be faster to implement and be more profitable in the long run. I'd like to take it on and partner with you on the project. I feel certain it'll be a huge success."

"You feel certain about Esme's idea."

Teresa nodded, tapping notes into her phone. "When you know, you know."

"I do know."

Leo looked down at Teresa. She had never once reached for his hand. It was always occupied with her phone. She had only twice looked him directly in the eyes before something else called her attention away. Meanwhile, when Esme was in the same room as him, he couldn't take his eyes off her. His hand itched even now to be filled with her.

"I can't wait to hammer out the details with you." Teresa practically bounced in her seat, scooting closer and holding out her handheld, pulling up a calendar. "When can you clear your schedule?"

"I suppose we'll be very busy planning the engagement and the wedding."

Teresa blinked, once, twice. "Right. Of course." She put her phone down and scooted back to her side of the car.

"You still want to get married?" he asked.

"Of course. Our union makes sense. We meet all the criteria of a strong partnership."

"You make us sound like business partners."

"We do make good business sense."

Leo chewed at the inside of his lip. "But not romantic sense?"

Teresa raised an eyebrow. "I didn't realize you were a romantic."

"I am," he said. "I just never got to show it."

"Of course not, being a royal. It's not a trait outside of fairy stories and romance novels. It's not our tradition. Royals are practical people. Everyone else gets to dream."

"What do you dream of, Teresa?"

She hesitated and then smiled sheepishly as she answered. "I dream of ships and the sea and charting new territories."

"So, this business deal between us, does it need to include romance?"

"I never expected to fall in love with the man I marry. I'll be a good wife. I like kids if you're worried about that. I'm willing to try for a son soon after the wedding, but I want to continue working during and after the pregnancy."

Lady Teresa would be good for Cordoba's future, that was clearly true. "Lady Teresa, I have a different proposition I'd like to present to you."

CHAPTER TWENTY-FOUR

"*A*nd the first place prize goes to ..."

The announcer twiddled his blonde mustache, dragging on the announcement of the winner of the pie maker contest in true showmanship fashion, but Esme wasn't truly paying attention. She hadn't tasted any of the pies. She hadn't even been there to help her friend make the pie. That had been left to Prince Alex who was gung ho in winning his rivalry against the duke.

The duke and his ringer stood confidently beside the announcer as if certain of their imminent victory. Alex and Jan stood on the other side. As the silence dragged on, Alex reached down and grabbed Jan's hand, lacing their fingers together.

Jan startled but didn't pull away from the prince. At any other time, Esme would be focused on that show of affection, ready to make it out to be more than it probably was. She'd let her imagination run away with her and start planning Jan and Alex's baby shower. But not today.

Esme's mind was still back on the docks, still watching Leo walk away hand in hand with the Duchess. It should have been her getting into that car with him. Or him staying behind on the docks with her. That was how the story was supposed to go.

The thing would've dictated nothing less. But Esme was starting to doubt that the thing had been there. Had she imagined it all? Had she seen what she wanted to fit the story she wanted to tell?

She'd cast herself as the heroine in this tale, but Leo had already written his name down in a different story. One that made no mention of her.

Esme hated to admit it, but the duchess was probably perfect for him. When Leo had mentioned this duchess last night after kissing Esme, she'd imagined a lemon-mouthed, wart-faced, stick of a woman. But that hadn't been the reality.

Lady Teresa was beautiful, with perfectly clear skin, and an hourglass figure. She was a nice woman, a capable woman, a true leader. The country would be lucky to have her. She wouldn't spill flour on the king's coat at dinner parties. She wouldn't destroy priceless statues.

But she also wouldn't love Leo the way that Esme did.

That she knew for a fact.

This wasn't how the storybook was supposed to go. But Esme wasn't living in a storybook world. The kindergarten teacher may have won the heart of the king, but she wasn't going to win his hand.

"The winner is Prince Alexander and Chef Peppers."

The room thundered in applause. The Duke clapped good-naturedly, while his Beard-award-winning chef tossed his mixing spoon and stormed out of the room. Alex swept Jan off her feet and dipped her back for a kiss.

Esme's claps paused in mid-air. Her own problems went out the window as she witnessed a new chapter in her friend's life taking shape. Maybe a common girl's fairytale was going to come true after all.

Jan wobbled when Alex set her back on her feet. His gaze didn't linger on her. No, he turned and high-fived the announcer, and then made his way around the crowd. Clearly, the kiss had no effect on him whatsoever.

That wasn't how that was supposed to go either. He was supposed to look into her eyes, and they were supposed to have a connection. The world was supposed to stop around them. Jan held still, but Alex was moving on.

"Well, that's over," Jan said when she made her way over to Esme.

In her hand, she held a check. It was why she'd come here, to further her career. Esme's reason for coming had been to realize a dream. A dream that was now playing out on the television screen overhead.

In the flat screen, the words Special Announcement blared on the screen. As the words dissolved, King Leo, dressed in the same suit he'd been in when she'd left him earlier, and Lady Teresa walked onto the screen. They weren't hand-in-hand. He had his arm at her back. And they were grinning like two toddlers who'd just found the snack jar.

"Citizens of Cordoba," Leo began. With the sound of his voice, the entire room went quiet and gave their attention to the television. "I am sorry to interrupt your broadcast and know the Geneva Jarvis talk show is far more entertaining than your monarch."

Polite laughter sounded from the audience before him in the conference room. It also sounded around the small ballroom the pie competition had been held in.

"As you know, Spain and Cordoba have had a long, sometimes contentious, other times beneficial, relationship for centuries. Lady Teresa of Almodovar and I have an announcement that we'll deliver later to night. It is an announcement that will greatly impact the future of our two great nations. I hope you will join me later this evening during the Union Day Gala to hear it live."

Leo turned to the duchess and smiled. She gave him a wink when she smiled back. Then the two turned and walked off the stage as reporters shot to their feet to ask questions which the two ignored.

The screen didn't fade to black. No, that was Esme's mind. Reporters came on to speculate about the announcement. The talk show host, Geneva Jarvis retook the airwaves. She and her guests wondered aloud if the announcement would be what everyone thought it would be, what was so obvious that it would be; an engagement announcement.

All Esme could think about was the look on Leo's face. He'd been smiling. He didn't look like his decision to turn his back on the thing had been a hardship at all. He looked excited.

"I think our adventure has come to an end," said Jan. "You ready to go home?"

"Yeah." Esme tried and failed to swallow past the lump in her throat. "Let's go home."

Esme hadn't remembered the trek to the west wing nursery. Her mind kept playing Leo's words over and over again in her head. Her mind looked for the loophole where she would be able to reinsert herself back into his life. Her heart searched for a way to return to his embrace.

Nothing came to her.

Inside the room, there was a rack of dresses fit for a grown princess. Esme assumed it was Alex's doing. He'd want Jan to look good tonight after their victory in the pie competition.

Jan hadn't even bothered to look at the gowns. She opened up her suitcase, which she had never entirely unpacked, and began shoving her toiletries inside. Esme walked over to the gowns.

She urged herself not to dream any more, not to let her imagination get away from her. There was no way she could go to that gala and hear the man she'd fallen in love with pledge his life to another woman. She had to get out of there. But when she turned to find her suitcase, she found a real live princess instead.

"Esme, look at my dress."

For the first time since she'd seen the little princess, Penelope wasn't in muted, pastel colors. She wore a deep, royal blue that made her eyes sparkle. Penelope's hair was done up in intricate swirls, and a small tiara crowned her head.

"Oh, Pen, you're as pretty as a princess."

"I am a princess." Penelope giggled.

When Esme had met the child, she didn't giggle. Now she was a happy five-year-old with a growing imagination. Esme couldn't help but wonder if she'd set this real live princess up for false expectations?

Would Penelope be allowed to write her own love story? Or would her father choose her husband for her?

"Why aren't you dressed?" asked Pen.

"We're not going to the ball."

"You're packing. Are you going home?"

Esme had done her best on this adventure. She'd put it all out on the table, and still, she'd lost. Not everyone wins.

"We have to get back to our jobs." Esme knew that was the perfect thing to say to the child who understood adult responsibilities at an early age. "Thank you so much for bringing me into your world, Penelope. I am so happy I got to meet you."

"We'll still be friends? Like you promised the other night?"

For the first time since Esme had known the little princess, her lip trembled. Esme brought Penelope into her arms. Esme might not be of royal blood, she might not win the hand of the king, but she had the heart of a princess, and that made her feel like a winner.

"You will forever be one of the dearest friends I have in my life," Esme said to the little girl.

"May I write to you?" Penelope asked when she pulled away.

"I would like that very much. How about I send you math problems and brain teasers?"

Of course, the little girl's eyes lit up as though Esme had promised her letters from Santa. Penelope turned to Jan. "And will you send me recipes for cookies and pies?"

"I definitely will," Jan said, coming over to give Penelope a hug of her own.

"And one day, you'll come back and visit again?" asked Penelope.

"One day," promised Esme.

She had fallen in love with the land of Cordoba. She would come back. One day. When it no longer hurt. She was sure that day was far, far away in the future.

CHAPTER TWENTY-FIVE

*L*eo straightened his tie in the mirror. He hardly recognized the person looking back at him. The man was smiling. There was a sparkle in his eye that he couldn't remember ever seeing before, not a single day in his life.

No, wait. He had seen that sparkle before. It had been reflected back to him whenever he looked into Esmeralda Pickett's bright gaze. He'd known the woman for less than a week, but already he couldn't imagine spending another day of his life without her.

"Here, let me help with that, your majesty." Giles obscured Leo's reflection and gave his tie a tug. "Tonight's announcement will mean great things for Cordoba."

"Yes, it will."

"You will secure the future of your countrymen for another generation, perhaps many more. All because you've made the right decision, the responsible decision."

"I agree, Giles."

For the first time in his life, Leo had made the right decision—for himself. He'd chosen to follow his heart but not until after he'd thought through all the ramifications with his head. He'd looked at the issue from every angle, made sure as many people would benefit as possible, and now he was ready to pull the trigger.

"Lady Teresa is a marvelous choice." Giles gave Leo's tie one more pat before moving away from the mirror. "She will make a great partner."

"Of that, I have no doubt." Now that Leo could see himself again, he had to admit the tie looked better under Giles's machinations.

"Your father would be proud of you."

Leo took a breath, his features screwed into a doubtful frown. "I'm not so sure about that. But I'm not looking to the past anymore. As you said, Cordoba has a bright future. That doesn't have to rest in the hands of a male. In the next parliamentary session, I'm introducing a bill to have the Primogeniture rights removed."

Giles blinked. "I ... I'm sorry, your majesty? Do you mean to say you wish to allow females the right to inherit the throne?"

"At five, Penelope has shown more leadership and intelligence than most nobles five times her age, my brother included. She deserves the right to rule if she chooses."

Giles frowned, and then to Leo's surprise, the man shrugged. "I actually can't find an argument with that."

"There will be other traditions brought up to the modern times as well. Brace yourself."

Leo left Giles standing in the mirror and headed down to the ballroom. The party was already in full swing. No one was dancing though a live band played. Servers moved about, offering small morsels and treats.

He searched the ballroom for Esme, not with his eyes, with his heart. He waited to sense her, certain that like magnets their gazes would connect. But there were far too many people crowded in the room for him to find her.

"You ready for this?"

Leo looked over to see Lady Teresa. She was dazzling in a light lavender gown. But she looked practically naked without a cellphone in her hand. Leo assumed it was in the tiny purse on her wrist.

His suspicions were confirmed when Teresa took his arm, and the purse was cradled between his rib and bicep. He felt the thing vibrating nonstop. She shrugged as though to say "What do you expect?" and he chuckled.

The room hushed as they made their way to the raised platform at the far end of the ballroom. All eyes were on them, but Leo's heart didn't pick up. He still hadn't found Esme's gaze. He took to the stage and gave one more glance, but didn't see her. Well, he knew that she would hear what he had to say.

"For centuries, Cordoba has flourished as a self-contained island nation. Now comes the time when we must reach outside our borders and welcome in the new. New people, new technology, new opportunities. It is with that thought in mind that I am announcing a partnership with Lady Teresa Nadal of Almodovar."

Applause sounded, glasses were raised, but Leo wasn't done. He'd only just got started.

"Nadal Shipping and Maritime Industrial have some exciting new technologies they want to bring forth to improve our oil refineries, along with exciting new innovations in shipping. But most excitingly, the Nadal family and Cordoba will start a line of luxury and family cruise ships. This new venture, which will be headed by Lady Teresa Nadal, will bring in new opportunities for current business growth, as well as new employment for

Cordovians young and old. My fellow citizens, please join me in celebrating this union."

There was a confused silence for a few beats. A few people had begun to clap, but it was a slow, golf clap that quickly died.

"Is that the only union you wish to announce, your majesty?" asked a member of the press. The man had a mic in hand and a cameraman at his shoulder.

Leo looked again out in the crowd, certain he'd find Esme walking towards him now that his announcement was complete, and his path to her was clear. But all he saw were the confused and expectant faces of the nobility and government officials. Where was she?

"I know many of you were hoping to hear of an engagement. Lady Teresa and I know that this is the best way we can partner. However, a special lady has captured my heart. She has helped me see the power of imagination. She has let me know that it is all right for my heart to dream. It all happened so fast, I find myself quite swept off my feet. She knows who she is, and if she is willing to come to my rescue, I'll happily ride off into the sunset with her."

There was a low murmur of excitement in the room now. This was what everyone had come for tonight, a love story not a business development. Still, no dark-haired, red-blooded American woman came forward.

Wait, no. The crowd began to part. Two figures moved forward.

But the two figures weren't a blonde pastry maker and a brown haired teacher whom Leo was hot for. Alex came forward with Penelope on his arm. They motioned for Leo to step to the side.

"What is it?" asked Leo. "Where's Esme?"

Alex took a deep breath. When he stalled, it was Penelope who delivered the news.

"Esme and Jan said it was time to head back to the real world. They left over an hour ago to take a flight back to America."

CHAPTER TWENTY-SIX

"Last call for Flight 377 direct to New York."

The line before the terminal gate had dwindled down to nothing. The elderly and disabled had boarded thirty minutes ago. Kids and their parents had already found their seats. Just a harried looking business man and a gruff backpacker remained in the line in front of Esme and Jan who hung back waiting until the last possible moment to board.

Esme looked down the hall of the terminal. There was no line at the men's bathroom, there never was. There was only one customer at the bar at this early evening hour. Two children ran around the empty seats on the other side of the terminal while their parents slumped in their seats.

"Final call," the flight attendant looked pointedly at Esme and Jan.

"Esme, we gotta go," said Jan, wheeling her luggage around.

Jan didn't say what they both were thinking. She didn't voice what was plain in the empty hallways. He wasn't coming.

Esme had seen enough dramas and romantic comedies. She'd read enough romance novels to know how the airport scene worked. The hero would come running through the airport terminal at the last second, dashing around travelers, leaping over luggage to arrive at the gate where his true love was just about to give up all hope and board the plane. He'd stop her and take her hand and profess his true and undying love before the haggard passengers.

Esme stood at the gate. Her boarding pass was in one hand. Her suitcase was in the other. Everyone had boarded, and not a soul was rushing down the hall. The last vestiges of hope left her on an exhale, and her shoulders deflated.

He wasn't coming.

Jan wheeled her case up to the annoyed attendant. *Beep* went her boarding pass, confirming that time was up. Esme stretched out her hand to give over her pass. But she jerked it back and turned once last time.

Perhaps he had gotten caught up at security. This traditional scene would likely suffer some technical issues in today's high security age where only ticketed passengers and guardians of minor travelers could enter the actual terminal.

But Leo was the king. This was his country. He was the final law.

And he was not coming.

Finally, Esme handed over her boarding pass. The *beep* was like the last blip of a heart monitor where the spike in the line signaled the end. It was the end of her fairytale. The last page of the book. And the tale had not ended well.

Maybe those kindergarten parents like Aubrey Thomas's mom were right. Maybe Esme shouldn't be reading the children fairytales. She'd read them all of her life and grown up believing. Leo and Penelope kept insisting that their lives weren't that of storybook fodder. But Esme had refused to believe them.

Duty and matters of state came before matters of the heart. A five-year-old got that lesson. Esme, a grown woman, was just now coming to face the fact.

Still, she couldn't be too disappointed. Penelope had developed a small sense of imagination. Hopefully, that would carry her through her life. And Leo ...

Well, he'd been loved by someone who'd wanted his happiness more than anything. And he'd loved her too, Esme was sure of it. She just needed to content herself with that part of the tale.

The past week of her life had been magic. She'd been rescued by a knight in shining armor. She'd journeyed to a faraway land. Slain a stone dragon. And even kissed a king.

Oh, that kiss. She'd felt like she could fly when he'd kissed her. And now she was being told to strap in for the journey back to earth.

"Goodbye Cordoba," she whispered looking out the plane's window. She saw the spire of the castle in the distance. It looked like a magical kingdom, and it was. But it was all grounded in reality.

"Girls like us live in the real world, Esme," said Jan. "But ... I will admit, there was a thing between you two."

Esme nodded as tears pricked her eyes.

"But a thing like that can't exist in the real world. Only in dreams."

"Leo was a dream come true."

"He's a good guy, but he has a job to do."

The plane began its taxi, and Esme's tears fell in earnest. She buried her face in Jan's shoulder as the plane accelerated and the wheels left the ground. Even before takeoff, Esme's heart dropped into her gut. It still couldn't let go of the dream that should've been.

Soon, the fasten seat belt signs went off. For a while, Esme kept hers on. She felt so restless and lightheaded that she needed to be tethered to something.

After thirty minutes in the sky, she needed to be free of the constraints. And so she rose and walked toward the front of the plane to the nearest bathroom. She didn't need to use the facilities. She just needed to move.

She couldn't shake that this was not how her story was meant to end. Part of her wanted to knock on the cockpit and tell the pilots to turn the plane around. And then what?

Leo had made up his mind. He was likely on the balcony kissing the duchess at this moment. Esme would have to move on.

But there would never be another king of her heart. A prince would no longer do. Even a knight would not suffice.

"Ladies and gentlemen," the pilot's voice rang over the intercom. "Please retake your seats. We will be making an unscheduled landing."

Esme snapped back to reality. Had she heard that right? She flagged a passing flight attendant.

"What's wrong?" Esme asked. "Is there an emergency?"

"Nothing to worry about, ma'am. We've just been ordered to land."

"Ordered? By who?"

"By the king."

CHAPTER TWENTY-SEVEN

*L*eo tapped his foot on the floor. He tugged at the strap of the seatbelt wanting desperately to be free. He knew the jet would outpace the commercial airline, but he needed to go faster. He needed to get to her this very moment.

"She's on an airplane," said Alex. "She can't escape you, though she tried."

The last part was said under his breath, but Leo heard his brother. Though Alex spoke in his typically droll fashion, Leo saw his brother drum his fingertips on the armrest. He was anxious too.

They had left the gala the moment Leo knew that Esme had gone. He was nearly an hour behind her. He'd pulled an uncharacteristic move when he'd used his power to halt all air traffic until his plane could take flight in pursuit of the woman he loved; the woman he needed to hold in his arms for the rest of his life.

What must she be thinking flying away from him? He hadn't told her that he loved her. Though there was definitely a thing between them, neither had verbalized it.

What if she hadn't truly known his feelings for her? He had denied those same feelings for duty. She was likely feeling horrible because of the choice he'd made. He just needed to get to her and rectify it.

He'd thought of calling her on the radio, but this needed to be done face to face. He needed to look her in the eye and tell her what a colossal idiot he'd been for not choosing her. His heart had chosen her, but his sense of duty had clouded his judgment.

That would be the last time. He was determined he would rule with his heart from this day forward. If he got to her in time.

"What if she's changed her mind?" he said. "I did walk away from her."

"Just toss her a tiara and a few jewels," said Alex. "She'll come running to your throne."

Leo sat up in his chair. He leaned forward, but the belt held him back. "She's not like that, and you know it. She liked me before she knew who I was, what I was. There's a thing between us."

Though Leo spoke with vehemence, his brother only grinned at him. Alex, who had unfastened the belt a moment before the light went off, reached over and patted Leo's knee. "Then sit back and relax. Your happy ending is on its way."

Easier said than done. "She's waited all her life to have her own fairytale, and I ruined her happy ending."

"Don't they call that in the books the Dark Moment? But here you are about to bring a silver lining. In full regalia no less. What woman wouldn't swoon?"

Leo looked down at himself. He'd rushed out of the castle without changing his clothes. Giles had been yelling after him about protocols and dry cleaning. Leo had ignored the man, so intent on following the love of his life.

Penelope had wished him luck, so had Lady Teresa. Would luck be enough? Could he play this by chance? It was just the rest of his life that was on the line.

"You'll have the rest of your life to make up for it," Alex was saying.

The rest of his life. The rest of their lives. He hoped so. He wanted to give Esme the world. He wanted to give her a fairytale.

Finally, the captain's voice came on the overhead with instructions to begin preparations for landing. The moment, the jet came to a stop at the terminal, Leo shot out of his seat. They'd landed at a private portion of the airport. The commercial side was on the other side of the air park.

Leo raced through the airport toward Esme's terminal. He dodged slow moving passengers and leapt over luggage trolleys. He'd move faster if he weren't in full regalia, but he had no choice.

And then he saw her. She was walking out of the arrival's gate with her suitcase bumping the back of her heels. Their gazes connected. Her mouth formed a perfect O. He could almost hear the gasp.

She didn't look at him in anger. She didn't turn away from him. Her face positively lit up. And there, there it was.

The thing.

It pulled him toward her like they were magnets. Like there was magic between them. He couldn't have fought the force if he'd tried.

Leo took a step forward ... and bumped into a traveler. The bump of his shoulder caused the man to lose his grip on his large suitcase. The case tumbled over, and a Chinese dragon spilled out.

The massive green head rolled over onto Leo's foot. The red, snaking tongue curled around his ankles. Leo tried to step over it, but his feet got tangled. He went down on one knee. But that didn't deter him.

He got to his feet, making quick work of the fake dragon until he was on the other side of the destroyed beast and in front of her; his tale-telling teacher, his irrepressible instructor, his starry-eyed scholar.

He needed to tell her how sorry he was he'd let her go. He needed to tell her that he couldn't imagine another moment without her. He needed to tell her he loved her. Leo opened his mouth, but nothing came out.

Esme waited patiently, expectantly while he fumbled their ending once more.

"I had everything I wanted to say to you planned in my head," he finally managed. "I just forgot all the words now that I'm looking at you."

"That's a good start," she said. "Did you just slay a dragon to get to me?"

"I would defeat any and everything that came between the two of us. I'm not sure if you're a damsel or a witch, because I came under your spell the first moment I laid eyes on you. I boarded a white jet and rode it hard to come to your rescue. And yes, I destroyed this man's dragon—which I will pay for, by the way—all to get to you."

She was in his arms, and Leo felt everything in his world shift. He came to realize that all his life he'd been looking at the world on a tilt. Now that the love of his life was finally in his arms, the balance was restored, and he saw the world anew.

"I nearly made the same mistake twice," he said. "I was ruling with my head instead of my heart. I was set to marry someone else, but I couldn't do it. See, there's this thing between you and me. I haven't encountered it before, so I wasn't sure if it could be what I thought it was. You're the expert in these types of stories, so you'll have to correct me if I'm wrong, but I think it's love."

"I know this story," she said. "I've studied it all my life. It's definitely a case of love."

"I love you, Esme. You are the queen of my heart."

"I love you too. But what about the country and the tradition?"

"The country will learn to love you as I do. You'll teach them, just as you taught me."

"I'm so glad you came. I almost gave up on fairytales."

"Not this tale. This is the only way this story could've ended."

Esme tilted her head to the left, and he went right. Their lips met in the middle in perfect alignment. Leo pressed his lips to Esme's and sealed their lips with a kiss to start the beginning of their happy ending.

$\mathcal{A}$lex looked at his brother and his soon to be sister-in-law and queen. He'd had more than his fair share of women offer their undying love to him. Watching Leo and Esme, Alex knew each of those women had been liars. Not one of those propositions came close to the bursting passion between those two.

For years, Alex had watched his brother toe the line. He'd had tried to lighten the load for Leo, but he usually wound up making a mess and more work for his overworked brother. With Esme in Leo's arms, Alex saw a definite lightening in his brother's shoulders.

Alex's gaze flicked to Jan on the other side of the couple. A rare smile peeked out of the corners of her lips. He knew Jan wasn't one for fairytales. The practical pie maker only had time to pair different spices. And she was a master at it.

He couldn't get the taste of her last dish out of his mouth. The woman was a wonder in the kitchen. He was glad she wasn't going away too soon. He couldn't wait to get her back into his kitchen.

Alex had his favorite dishes. But no one had ever made

him want to try the same dish twice in a row on the same day. But Jan did.

She'd only made him desserts. He wondered what a side dish under her mixing spoons might taste like. He wondered if he might coax her into making a main dish? Perhaps even a full course if she stuck around?

Despite his parents barring him from the castle's kitchens when he was younger, Alex loved the world of food. He'd had to indulge his passions away from his homeland and spent most of his time on food expeditions to the far reaches of the world tasting exotic dishes. Jan was the first woman he'd met that shared that passion.

He wanted to show her his private spice collection and see what she'd make of it. He wanted to cook beside her and come up with new mixtures. Yes, he definitely wanted to watch her work in the kitchen again. Perhaps she might even consider a partnership with him?

Alex was tired of being known as the playboy prince, as the directionless spare. He had an idea, an idea that made him excited. An idea that made his mouth water. And Jan was the one, the only one who could bring his vision to light.

He went around the kissing couple and stood next to Jan. "Hey."

She eyed him suspiciously. She'd done that since the first day they'd met. She was a smart girl.

"I suppose you'll be catering the wedding reception?" he said.

With a tiny shake of her shoulders, she laughed. It was a pleasant sound. He'd heard it while she'd prepared the winning pie the other day. He caught a whiff of sweetness from her breath on his tongue.

It wasn't the sweetness of her winning pie. It was the

sweetness he'd tasted when he'd stolen a kiss from her when they'd won the competition. The kiss had meant nothing. Except that he couldn't get it off his mind.

"Before wedding plans get underway, I have a proposal of my own. For you."

"What kind of proposal?"

**To find out what plan Alex has cooked up for the pie maker,
be sure to grab your copy of
*The Prince and the Pie Maker!***

ABOUT THE AUTHOR

Shanae Johnson was raised by Saturday Morning cartoons and After School Specials. She still doesn't understand why there isn't a life lesson that ties the issues of the day together just before bedtime. While she's still waiting for the meaning of it all, she writes stories to try and figure it all out. Her books are wholesome and sweet, but her heroes are hot and heroines are full of sass!

And by the way, the E elongates the A. So it's pronounced Shan-aaaaaaaa. Perfect for a hero to call out across the moors, or up to a balcony, or to blare outside her window on a boombox. If you hear him calling her name, please send him her way!

You can sign up for Shanae's Reader Group at http://bit.ly/ShanaeJohnsonReaders

ALSO BY SHANAE JOHNSON

The Rebel Royals series

The King and the Kindergarten Teacher

The Prince and the Pie Maker

The Duke and the DJ

The Marquis and the Magician's Assistant

The Princess and the Principal

www.ingramcontent.com/pod-product-compliance
Lightning Source LLC
Chambersburg PA
CBHW071802190726
48292CB00008B/2684